The Master of Fate

The Master of Fate

Gonzalo Munevar

Black Heron Press
Post Office Box 95676
Seattle, Washington 98145
http://mav.net/blackheron

The Master of Fate has been awarded the 1999 Black
Heron Press Award for Social Fiction

AJE-3202
193

FEB 0 9 2000

The Master of Fate is a work of fiction. Any resemblance to
persons living or dead is purely coincidental.

ISBN: 0-930773-55-1

Cover art and design: Cami Lemke

Published by:
    Black Heron Press
    Post Office Box 95676
    Seattle, Washington 98145
    http://mav.net/blackheron

For Hernando

1

Bogota, damn you Bogota! How I hated you that cold and foggy morning on the soccer field of the Calasanz School for Men. "You will be the pride of your family, of your school, of your country," the principal of the provincial school had said to me in public. And so my parents had sent me to boarding school in the capital, to prove myself, with my younger brother Homero, who would have been far happier moving with the rest of the family to our new home in Cartagena. We thought about that city on the Caribbean coast as we shivered and waited for the school year to begin. Damn you Bogota! A whistle pierced the fog and we joined the many other bodies that converged toward the classroom building. Under the front doorway Homero and I glanced briefly at each other and went our separate ways. We were so young—two to three years younger than most of the classmates we were about to meet. When I walked into the classroom a priest stopped me and asked me, "Do you really belong in the fourth form of secondary, child?"

Not an auspicious beginning. But in a few minutes the sun would break through, my new classmates would make me feel welcome, and everything around me would be colored by hope. How quickly my confidence grew. And how misguided!

What went wrong? I soon learned my way around the boarding school and, already in that very February of '59, I thought that I could conquer all, that my life could be limited only by the bounds of my ambition and my dreams. In retrospect that confidence was not entirely unwarranted. So what went wrong? I wish I could understand. I need to understand why nothing matters, why I no longer care. I walk aimlessly about the cold and rainy city, I observe it from its ugly, filthy entrails. Goddamned Bogota! I walk its gray, endless streets while trying to remember, to remember so I can understand. I need to tell my own story, to make sense of my own story. I must do this on my own because my books—and what they represent—have forsaken me. Of what use can the myths of modern psychology be, for example? By having my memories twisted into a formula of infantile incest and problems with toilet training, or something just as fanciful, I will end up with a tale not my own, with a fabrication that will belong to no one. I might even come to believe that I understand. But it will not be my life, not the life of Oscar Moreira, not the life of that boy, not yet fourteen, who waited in the cold fog with his brother Homero, blades of grass sticking to our wet shoes, for the new school year, for a new life to begin.

No, in my protected life up to that point, I was what might be called "well adjusted." And whatever apprehensions I might have had prior to the school year faded away quickly. In the previous months I had formed an image of authoritarian Spanish priests awakening us at five in the morning to take a cold shower, hurrying us to make our beds in military style, leading us to dimly lit dining rooms where we would stand in line for our daily rations of swill, an image of all those pleasant character-building niceties ("will make men out of you," my father had said) that one could expect from a boarding school. Thus I could not be unhappy later on that first day, as I sat at my assigned table in that dining room of high ceilings, tall windows, and bright colors, as the waiter served me seconds of that hardy and appetizing food, as I looked across the clean white table cloth and the sparkling china and engaged my three table mates in easy conversation.

Nor was I exhausted by that time, as I had feared, for the morning began at a reasonable hour actually, with a nice, hot shower. And then—to top it all—the maids made the bed. As for the Escolapian priests who ran the school, far from being authoritarian—with a couple of exceptions—they were friendly and informal. That first letter home was going to be a good one!

No, something happened after that, although I suspect I must begin my story at that time, when it looked as if the realization of the promise within me had just began. How I wish that this story were not necessary, that I could find the required wisdom in the vast treasures of literature. But I search in vain. So many tales of woe, yet none seem to apply. Characters rise from the ruins of their souls, face up to their tragedies and as a consequence achieve peace, insight, redemption, or perhaps just plain maturity. So many things that characters achieve. But there are no concentration camps in my past, no horrors of war, no murder, no crippling accidents, no betrayal of incendiary love, no extraordinary episodes of any kind. Nor am I enlightened by stories in which the character "finds himself," for it puzzles me more to know how the character could be in the position that necessitated his voyage of self-discovery in the first place. No. Mine could not be a story about the building of character, but about its erosion, about the slow accumulation of small forces and events that ultimately dries the soul and leaves the heart empty.

This may be too melodramatic a beginning. If I claim not to care, not to feel, why should I say that I need to tell my own story, to understand, and so on. But this is just a manner of speaking; it is more accurate, but also more cumbersome, to say that I think I should care, I should feel, but that I cannot unless I understand what has happened to me. So the task ahead is not the painting of rich melodrama but rather the surrealistic drawing of distorted lives melting on arid landscapes. If my ends are to be served, this must be a clinical examination, at times perhaps even brutal. It is not enough to know that my life is distorted, I must also know how it is distorted. To draw with sympathy may undermine my very purpose. To color with poignancy may forever falsify the very object I am trying to illuminate. Excuses are so easy to accept. I have no choice: my own light must shine harshly, it must leave no place to hide.

My only initial problem seemed to be that I had great difficulty understanding the Spaniards' accents. I finally had to tell Professor Reyes, my geometry teacher, about it and from then on he would finish his explanations by saying "Has Moreira understood?" With Father Francisco—Pancho—the Prefect of Discipline, there was no such problem: his clear, booming voice would carry anywhere, startling wrongdoers and imposing order in every corner of the school. I always watched my step in his anatomy class, as well as everywhere I suspected his small but imposing presence. At first I thought that clear Spanish accents went with rather unfriendly temperaments. There was Father Jorge—"The Ogre"—the head of the boarding section, for example. He was young, skinny, long-nosed, and wore thick glasses and a constant frown. Every night before bedtime he spoke to us about duty, restraint, persistence and other such edifying topics. Students would snicker at him behind his back, but as time went on I found his little chats rather pleasant. And as I did increasingly well in anatomy class I came to suspect that Pancho was a bit paternal and that he might even think well of me. The other Escolapians were easy to like.

My greatest enthusiasm was reserved for Father Miguel, the priest who had initially embarrassed me with his question about the propriety of my presence in the fourth form. He was handsome and witty, was always interceding on the students' behalf with the rest of the faculty, and in general made himself our friend and patron saint. And he seemed to enjoy a good round of teasing. He, like most of the other Escolapians, was a fanatic follower of Franco; so we would make fun of his hero and go on at length about dictators and fascist leftovers. He would mumble something about uncivilized savages not being able to comprehend great historical missions, egging us on to counterattack.

"You Spaniards are a bunch of thieves," we would say. "You came and stole all the gold from South America. Now you begrudge us our being poor. Of course we are. After you carried away everything we had."

"You're ungrateful," he charged, "you shouldn't insult the name of Spain after she gave you your culture and your religion."

"Some culture, the most backward in the world."

"I wouldn't say that. And, besides, if you wish to call us thieves, just remember that you are descendants from the people the kings sent here, and that those people were the worst of Spain: thieves, murderers, Jews. If you want to talk about thieves you should remember the kind of blood that flows in your veins."

"That's a lie! Only the best from Spain cane here, that's why they had to get a certificate of good conduct before they could come."

"If you were robbed, it happened because you were fools."

One of my table mates, Ochoa, who was always bragging about his sexual adventures, came up with the story that Father Miguel had not only one but several girlfriends, naturally, his being so handsome. I didn't believe him. Neither did the others, I Imagine. But it added to Father Miguel's mystique. Nevertheless, my greatest enthusiasm for Father Miguel stemmed from the promise implicit in his apologetics class: he was going to offer us a rational defense of religion. Like most of us, he said, he had once been beset by doubts, but obviously he had overcome them. That, I thought, was the greatest service El Calasanz could offer me: to rid me of those nagging questions about the existence of God. And it was good also to know that I was not alone in my predicament, that those around me experienced the same disquieting thoughts.

Those remarks by Father Miguel made me feel closer to my classmates, or at least to some of them. The fourth form was divided into two sections, of about twenty-five students each. And my section was itself informally divided into two groups. I belonged to the soccer group, which was led by Hoyos and Pinto. We played during every recess, and in general whenever we had a chance. And when we didn't play we argued about our favorite teams. Pinto was the chief supporter of Santa Fe, I of Millonarios. For three entire years we played and played, and we argued. The more "serious" members of the class had their own group and thought us rather immature. They only talked about adult matters. But during the study periods they would take the ball away from us and throw it all over the room, bouncing it off the heads of those who studied or slept. Once in a while some indignant victim would throw the ball out the window and we had to muster the ingenuity to recover it before Pancho did.

To the "serious" group belonged Ochoa, who was as old with respect to the class as I was young (some people said as old as twenty), and another of my table mates, Iriarte, a redhead from Cali. Not that Iriarte had anything against soccer. He was the best player in the class, and perhaps in the entire school. I liked him, not only because he was always friendly to me, but because I found him amusing at the dining table. It was very common for him to start the table conversation with some bizarre statement. One day, for example, he said to Ochoa, "Did you know that Boada's sister is a whore?"

"You mean she is easy?"

"No. A whore. A streetwalker."

"Aw, come on!"

"Ask him if you don't believe me."

"I can't ask him something like that!"

"I'll do it myself then."

Iriarte turned to Boada, who was at the next table. "Boada! Hey, Boada!" he shouted. "These guys don't believe me that your sister is a streetwalker. Tell them."

"Yes," Boada said. "She and Iriarte's sister work together."

Iriarte shrugged his shoulders. "He got me there." Then he began to eat his soup.

One big topic of conversation that year was the Jew. The Jew came into the lunchroom late that first day, but there had been advance word of his arrival and immediately all eyes were set in his direction. He was tall, skinny, pale, with a long nose, and kinky hair.

"That's what all Jews look like," Ochoa said. "One can tell by the nose and the hair."

"I don't think so," Iriarte argued. "I know many of them and they look just like anybody else."

Apparently, however, many of us had never seen a Jew before. He first became a victim of curiosity and then—when he reacted against the general attitude—of malice. By supper time he had already been in two fights. He was not only beaten up but nicknamed. "Ugly as a fetus!" The insult ricocheted throughout the dining room and by dessert almost everybody was scoffing at the Fetus.

The Jew slept only two beds away from Homero, whose bed was next to mine. The first night, when the lights went out someone shouted, "Smells like fetus around here." The Jew's reply was drowned by the laughter of the twenty or so students in the dormitory.

Soon enough his situation become impossible. "Have you heard the latest about the Fetus?" would run from table to table in the dining room. Someone had put a tack on his seat, a padlock on his desk, had pushed him out of formation in front of Pancho who, thinking he was clowning, had punished him. Sometimes the Jew would push back or express doubts about the joker's ancestry, which only increased his persecutors' viciousness. And the Jew would isolate himself even more, head bowed over his meal. Once in a while he would raise his big black eyes, bright with hate, or perhaps with pain.

Unlike the Jew, I felt very pleased with life in El Calasanz.

In the thick, solid walls of the buildings I saw a guarantee of warmth and security. And on the soccer field I could let myself go completely in my pursuit of the great pass, of the deciding goal. I also loved most of my classes and at night would relish doing the homework. During an evening study period, Father Jorge stopped by the side of my desk. He smiled at me. "You're a good boy," he said. I thought that he really wasn't as bad as people claimed. Yes, things were going well then. And not only for me. I could see that my brother Homero was also flourishing. We even stopped wishing that our parents had taken us to Cartagena. We wrote them about our good life instead.

After lunch on Saturday, we had several free hours for sports or reading. At four in the afternoon they showed movies to us and the boarders from the Calasanz for Women. The girls sat on one side and we on the other. Unfortunately we never had occasion to talk to them.

On Sunday we slept in late. After Mass we went on a trip. Sometimes they took us picnicking to the lowlands, other times to a soccer game. The stops at the ice cream parlor were frequent. At night we watched tv until it was time to go to bed.

Acouple of weeks after the beginning of school our grandfather Humberto Moreira took us to see Millonarios play against Santa Fe. To my great distress, Santa Fe won on a lucky goal by the center forward. This gave the soccer group in my class an opportunity to tease me for weeks.

Of course, after a while the situation began to fall a bit short of ideal. Father Miguel's apologetics class was not living up to my hopes. St. Anselm's proof for the existence of God seemed ludicrous, for example, and my exchanges about it with Father Miguel were becoming exasperating. "Father, I don't see the sense of saying that the idea of a perfect being implies that it exists. Let's suppose that I imagine a perfect dog; according to your reasoning it must exist because if it didn't it wouldn't be perfect."

"That is not the point at all, Moreira. I don't know what's the matter with you. Perhaps if you tried to see things with a little more faith it wouldn't be so hard for you to understand."

I decided to take my doubts to Father Jorge instead. His room was next to my dormitory. "Come in," I heard his voice from inside. "What a pleasant surprise." The room was rather large and Spartan, the furniture plain and cheap. "Sit down." He offered me a chair by the desk and then sat next to me.

"In spite of the loss to Santa Fe, Millonarios is the best," he said. How could he know it was so important to me? I was surprised.

"Panzutto's goal was sheer luck," I commented. He smiled.

"And what else brings you around here?" He placed his hand on my shoulder, which annoyed me.

"Well, Father, I want to talk to you about a problem I have." The pressure of his hand made me ill at ease, but I didn't know how to get rid of it. He waited for me to continue.

"I have doubts about the existence of God, Father."

"You shouldn't worry; the same thing has happened to all of us at some time in our lives, particularly during our youth. It's natural. When we grow up the doubts disappear."

"But what am I going to do in the meantime, Father?" I wished that he would remove his hand.

"Father Miguel's course should help you in the meantime."

"But it isn't helping, Father. I still can't buy that some Being created for our benefit everything we see."

"But someone must have created it, right?"

"But why, Father? Why?"

"Have you ever seen anything that doesn't have a cause? Everything has a cause, and the cause of all causes is God."

"But what is the cause of God?"

"God has no cause because He is God."

"That's what I don't see, Father. If the world must have a cause, why mustn't God?"

"Look," he said, taking his arm away, which I really appreciated, "I am going to lend you a very good book. I think it may help you. Better still, I'll give it to you as a present." He began to look for it among a pile of books spread on top of his dresser. "Here it is." Its title: *Power and Purity*. I thanked him and went to bed.

He was alone in the room and the idea came to him. A few days earlier some friends had told him about it. He undressed slowly, pondering what he was about to do. Yielding to the force of the flesh, he gave himself, finally, to the solitary sin.

Passages of that sort abounded in the book Father Jorge had given me. Later would follow details on the moral degradation of the individuals who thus left the "good path." And then apocalyptic visions of terrible illness and other punishments that befell the transgressors of the natural and divine laws.

The most pathetic case was that of a man who had dedicated himself to the "solitary sin" in his youth and thus contracted a venereal disease that affected his eyesight. Years later all his children were born blind and the poor repentant sinner continuously wept over his weakness of will during his younger years.

The book placed great emphasis on the sins of the flesh as the main cause of atheism: One became an atheist in order to excuse his bad behavior. The other two causes were ignorance of Christ's principles and false pride. The book did not help me at all because my situation did not seem to resemble any of the cases offered as evidence. The solitary sin intrigued me, however. I realized that one could commit the sexual act with other men rather than with women, as it was said of the Vallians, or with animals, as was unfortunately alleged of the people from the Coast. But with himself?

I finally decided to ask Father Jorge.

He was dumbstruck for a long while. "You really don't know?" he finally said.

"No, Father, I simply can't imagine it."

He looked at me in silence again, letting his hand wander through my hair. "You are truly surprising. Perhaps it would be better for you not to find out yet."

Evidently he sensed that I was not satisfied, for he went on. "If you don't know what the solitary sin is you can't commit it, can you? So you are better off not knowing."

"Perhaps you are right, Father," I told him. What a long, skinny nose he has, I thought. Should I tell him that I didn't like to be touched? His fingers kept on playing with my hair while he explained how unusual and valuable was a fourteen-year-old boy who still preserved his purity.

"You have never gone to bed with a woman, have you? No. Of course not."

"No, Father."

"Perhaps it will surprise you, but at least half your class.... I wish we had more boys of your caliber at this school."

A few weeks later I received a package from Cartagena: my birthday cake. That night I distributed it in the dormitory. Father Jorge brought some consecration wine and we all made a party of it—followed by a general pillow fight as soon as Father Jorge retired. I was finally fourteen, but many of my classmates still treated me as a little boy. Ochoa—in particular—after each of his dirty jokes at the table would make some remark about "innocence" and would remind himself that he shouldn't tell such stories in front of me even if I couldn't understand them. I am sure he was the one who nicknamed me "little angel." His favorite topics were French movies and his sexual adventures whose descriptions he exaggerated until I called him immoral. He would then say something about "maturity" or simply smile at me with superiority and satisfaction. I suspected every time that he was setting a trap for me, but I would nonetheless fall for it.

It was infuriating to see him take communion every day. I didn't feel I had enough of a right to receive the sacraments and yet he put on such pious airs that one would expect him to levitate at any moment. During one of my frequent visits I mentioned to Father Jorge that Ochoa was a hypocrite and the priest agreed with me.

I was not really bothered, however, by all the teasing about my age. I was used to it, on the one hand, and I was actually proud of being ahead of my years, on the other.

Homero, who was in the same boat, found things even easier because he looked older than his age, and in addition could be very tough in a fight, when someone tried to push him too far.

As Easter vacation neared we took our first important examinations. I was rather concerned about my performance because, as my mother had said, "El Calasanz is a really serious school." It is true that I felt at ease in most classes, but being new I couldn't be all that confident. And then there were the two Colombian professors, who simply did not measure up to the Spaniards. One of the two taught us philosophy. He always seemed embarrassed about his subject matter. Upon learning, for example, that Thales of Miletus had claimed that the world was made of water, we would make fun: "Not the whole world, Colombia is made of beer." He then reacted as if it were his fault that we found Thales stupid.

The other Colombian was Piggy, our English and French instructor. He was a short, chubby man with an enormous head. His eyes were small, and his thick face sported the sort of mustache that Hitler made infamous. Piggy wasted no time in becoming the laughing stock of the entire school. His very first day he walked into a classroom and immediately—without provocation—delivered a most threatening harangue, only to find out that he was not just in the wrong classroom but on the wrong floor altogether. When he finally came to us, he said that he was going to "tame" us. It is amazing that anyone would say such things. But Piggy did. Right before our first English exam he announced that he had been with Scotland Yard for seventeen years and there was no chance that cheating would go undetected by him. The cheating that went on that day! And more out of daring than out of necessity, I would suspect.

Piggy was a joke, but he was a vindictive joke. And he had accumulated a long and rather inaccurate list of what he called "saboteurs." He was convinced, rather perceptively, that the students had declared war on him. People destroyed his classes by laughing, singing, fighting, or playing tricks on the teacher. Neither his threats nor Pancho's frequent punishments changed things much.

There were many unknowns, then, and I awaited the results of the examinations anxiously. A detestable guy named Ruiz was expected to take first place. Because of an illness at the end of the previous year he had to repeat the fourth form, and now he kept telling us how easy it was for him. He also gave himself grand society airs, talked continuously of his family's money and the Country Club, and despised the rest of us for not being as rich and intelligent. We hated him. And when the time came we hated to see him take first place. But I placed second and that made me very happy. It was not a bad start. My parents would be proud.

2

Cartagena was my native city but I had no memory of it. As the DC-4 flew us home I tried to picture the city of castles on the shores of the Caribbean, tried to picture the sea. My mother had told me of my adventures on the beach, but my only images of the sea came from photographs and movies. It had been a long time. But now I was coming home. The noise from the engines turned into a reassuring murmur...invited sleep. My native city at last...after so many moves....we resembled gypsies: from a plastics factory in one town to a steel mill in another, and so on, forever in search of a more promising job for my father somewhere else...my father was a gypsy with a degree in chemical engineering...he now worked with a government-owned petrochemical company...he was the production manager...the type of position he had wished for all his life...perhaps we wouldn't have to move again...my native city, my new city, strange city.... The noise from the engines became more strident, the plane felt tauter, as a muscle right before the decisive play. It began to descend. We would be there in only a few minutes.

Our family would be waiting for us at the airport. My father, tall and strong, a serious expression on his face, watching my mother pamper baby Ruben, a year and a half, making some remark about it. My mother's young, beautiful face answering with an ironic smile—she well knew that he pampered the baby more than anyone else. And the little one would be saying "'ane" every time an airplane took off or landed. My sister, Dora, would want a comic book. The DC-4 broke through a veil of clouds and the Caribbean Sea pressed its blueness against my eyes. My father would be paying for the drinks, his white face already showing the effects of the coastal sun. My sister would want a chocolate....

The wing on my side first pointed toward the dwarf waves down below, and finally leveled off, almost at sea level. On the horizon the water gave way to a spot of yellow, of sand, that grew, that became beach, that in turn gave way to the long blackness of the runway.

We quickly went down the portable staircase and stepped on Cartagenian soil. At the gate a forest of black faces and short-sleeved white shirts stirred in expectation of the passengers. Once through the noisy crowd we found ourselves in our mother's arms, being hugged and kissed without end. Even Dora hugged and kissed us. My father patted our backs, asked us a thousand questions about the trip, and in general made his pleasure evident. Baby Ruben found a place in Homero's arms and was carried in them until we got the luggage. As we drove home my father told us the names of neighborhoods, churches, hills, castles, too many names to remember. We went by some fortifications from colonial times, their ancient cannons raising their black mouths among the palm trees. Across the road we could see the miserable slums where descendants of the slaves who built the forts rotted away.

We entered Bocagrande, the neighborhood of the rich, and forgot about poverty. In Bocagrande the houses were beautiful and the gardens lush with tropical exuberance. My neighborhood. And everywhere the sea. My sea. My native city.

I looked right and left with satisfaction, took my coat off and was grateful for the coastal heat that revived me, laughed at the baby's playful noises, and answered my mother that yes, I was happy. My father drove the car into the driveway of a new two-story house and announced that we were home. "Really? What a beautiful house," Homero and I said almost in unison, bringing a smile of satisfaction to his face. We stood in front of the house admiring its gardens, its large picture window, its green walls, its white porch over the garage.

"The Company rented this house for your father," my mother told us later. "Here they know how to appreciate what he's worth." Inside, the house was as spacious and full of light as the exterior had promised. In the morning the living room would be illuminated by a light that arrived green after crossing the front yard and garden. In the afternoon the dining room filled with the colors of the backyard: soft and deep greens, clear beiges and whites, golds, blues, violets and bright reds, the colors of palm trees, coconuts, papayas, guanabanas, mangoes, and climbing flower plants. Toward dusk, when the air conditioning was no longer needed, I liked to go up to my room on the second floor, open the window, lie down on my bed, and let the breeze slowly curl in with the scents of so many fruits and flowers while I thought about everything and nothing. I would remain there until the crickets heralded the darkness, and then I would join the rest of the family on the porch to watch the last few moments of sunset, to talk, to hear my mother's kidding and my father's projects for the future, to wait for dinner to be served.

The day after our arrival we went back to the airport to receive my Uncle Fabio, his wife Elena, and their daughters Inez and Ester. Accompanying them was a very good-looking red-haired woman. "Pleased to meet you, Miss," I said, and offered to help with her luggage. She laughed merrily and I felt disconcerted. "Don't be stu-

pid," my mother told me later, "she is Justina, their maid."
Uncle Fabio embraced my mother: "Agh, I'm sorry to see
you in this condition, little sister. You look so old that
anyone would take you for my mother."

"Fabio!" Aunt Elena seemed embarrassed.

"You idiot," my mother said to him. She hugged
him back. "Happy are the eyes that see you." She looked as
young and beautiful as ever. I had once shown my wallet
to my table mates and they had been especially attracted to
a picture of my mother sitting in a garden.

"What a great looking broad," Iriarte said. "Where
did you get her?"

"She's my mother."

"Your mother!" Ochoa had exclaimed.

There were hugs and "hi's" to suffice everyone,
and curious looks between our cousins and us. Inez was a
bit older than I, had brown hair, blue eyes, and a "complete body," as Homero later remarked to me. Ester was
Homero's age, blonde, also blue-eyed, as reserved as her
mother, and her body was just beginning to develop. At
night Homero and I took a long inventory of them, always
adding "Unfortunately they are cousins." But nonetheless.... We were very conscious of the maid Justina, but for
some strange reason felt very inhibited when thinking of
her and so we seldom mentioned her.

We barely stopped at the house to leave the luggage and then went for a drive around the city. To the San
Felipe Castle, a colonial fortress almost the size of a moun-
tain. There we learned of Inez's great passion for photog-
raphy. We took pictures in front of old cannons, in a
smiling group perched on a lookout, sitting on a sentinel's
court. Pictures of Inez, engineered by Inez, the face pen-
sive, absorbing the breeze, observing the city from the
historical heights, the expression cautious, inspecting the

entrance to one of the many tunnels of the castle. Pictures, later, of the two families taking refreshments by the swimming pool of the Hotel Caribe. Pictures of Uncle Fabio squatting beside the Shoes of the Poet. Pictures of a shipwreck half sunk in the bay. Pictures of an ancient convent on the top of a very high hill. Pictures of the city from the convent.

Uncle Fabio had come on business, and my father had to work all week long. Whenever both of them had some free time we would take long trips: by boat to Bocachica, by car to the southeast—on a picnic and a visit to the petrochemical plant where my father worked. Homero and I were a bit disappointed by the small size of the installation. My father noticed and hastened to explain that the company was just beginning and that in a few years it would be the most important of its kind in South America.

When the heads of family were working, the rest would go downtown—an exotic mixture of colonial buildings, fortresses built against the pirates, stone-paved streets, and new stores—to shop or visit museums and monuments. Or else we would go to the beach two blocks away from our front door, or to the swimming pool at the Hotel Caribe three blocks away.

The first time we went to the beach my mother teased Aunt Elena for allowing my cousins to wear bikinis. "It is very fortunate for these girls, Elena, that in spite of your prudishness and all you don't bother them."

"You really kid a lot, Julia. It's plain that you are Fabio's sister."

Homero and I were, of course, quite pleased.

"I am so amazed," my mother said, "about how quickly Inez has grown into a lady. She must have a steady boyfriend already."

"Aunt Julia!" Inez blushed. But she was obviously flattered. A lady. That's how she behaved. Ester imitated her, without grace. Dora observed them both and tried to follow in their footsteps. "Miss Dora," Homero would call her and she would look at him with loathing.

"I hope you'll give these girls all the breaks they deserve," my mother went on. "When I finished high school, Humberto was studying engineering at La Javeriana, so naturally I wanted to stay in Bogota. I begged my father to let me enroll in La Javeriana but the damned old miser refused."

"Julita, how can you speak that way of your father?"

"But, Elenita, the whole world knows the old man is tighter than a sailor's knot. When I asked him for the tuition money he went into such a fit that he ended up bald just from pulling out his own hair."

"Julita!"

"In any event, I didn't want to stay in Pereira like an idiot, waiting for Hernando to finish school. What was I to do? Become a maid in my parents' house? It would've been so boring that I might have turned into a piece of furniture. No, dear. Besides, I truly wanted to go to school. So I kept insisting to the man with the money. He kept refusing, claiming that college was not an appropriate place for women. One day I asked him why and he yelled that if God had meant for women to go to college He would have given them some brains inside their heads. Can you imagine?"

"But didn't you attend La Javeriana?"

"Sure. By making his life so miserable and by having my mother—bless her soul—cry oceans on my behalf. He finally sent me to study languages. When I married, long before graduation, he was very upset over all the money he had wasted on my college education."

Her own story made my mother think that it was time to discuss my future "seriously." Now that we were in boarding school in Bogota and doing well (Homero had placed third in his class), we were no longer treated as little boys but as serious men. Mister Oscar Moreira, Mister Homero Moreira. Since I was older and had better grades than Homero I was more of a man and more serious. Dignity went to my head and I walked around with my face twisted into a frown of maturity. One morning Uncle Fabio asked me whether by mistake someone had put starch on my face rather than on my shirt. I didn't think it was at all funny.

My father told me that I could major in the subject of my choice at the university of my choice once I finished high school. But when I mentioned that I was interested in astronomy, he seemed a bit disappointed that I didn't have my heart set on becoming a chemical engineer. But soon he recovered and suggested the possibility of my studying abroad.

I took great pleasure in noticing how tall, good looking, intelligent, sure of himself, how imposing my father was. I was his son, his heir. I would be like him. Someday.

Someday. In the meantime he explained to me the history of the Cartagenian castles, the strategic position of the fortresses with respect to the invading pirates, the relationship between the Intercol refinery and the petrochemical plant for which he worked, the best way of navigating the bay by small boat, the different types of ship owned by the Colombian navy. In the meantime he took us here and there, gave us money for movies and ice cream and promised more for model airplanes and boats.

In the meantime we played tennis at night with him and Uncle Fabio. In the meantime he smiled at the onslaught of my mother's kidding, and by gestures asked us not to pay attention to her.

Who would have known!

From spending too much time on the beach I got a tremendous sunburn. It seemed as if every piece of skin that had not been covered by my trunks was peeling off by the fistful. While the others went swimming I stayed home smeared with white ointments, prepared to withstand the pain stoically, in keeping with my newly acquired maturity. After a while I heard Justina's laughter in the backyard and went to the window to look at her. What a surprise when I saw her completely nude, playing among the palm and fruit trees! Though not as great as the surprise at seeing my uncle Fabio after her. She was laughing, he was beginning to take his clothes off. She eluded him, for play's sake. He grabbed her, kissed her. His hands, his lips traveled through her bright red hair, over her very white skin. She laughed. What laughter! What a beautiful body! He told her things. She laughed some more. They finally disappeared from my sight, went to her room. I looked at the yard once again: It seemed incredible that Justina had been there in the nude, sensual, playful, among the papaya trees, the coconut trees, among the flowers and the trunk of the guanabana just a few seconds earlier. Even more incredible that she was no longer there, as if it were not possible that the yard could go on existing without the wonderful nakedness of her body.

I remained disturbed for some time, but decided to exercise my adult will and forget what had happened. That same night, however, when I was sitting in the living room waiting for everybody else to get ready for the movies, she came close to me, ran her fingers through my hair and said, "My, what a cute boy." How could I ever get her out of my mind?

3

Upon our return to El Calasanz we found the Jew determined not to let any abuse at all go unchallenged. Bunking so close together, a confrontation with Homero became practically inevitable. "Hey, Fetus," my brother said to him one evening. "You've been stinking up this side of the dormitory for a long time. When are you going to take a shower, you pig?"

The Jew started pushing my brother, who wasted no time in knocking him to the ground. Homero then turned around and began to go about his business when all of a sudden he heard the Jew call him aloud.

"Moreira! You son-of-a-bitch!"

Homero turned around, his fists ready, only to confront the mouth of a small pistol. The dormitory came to a dead stop.

We all stared at the pistol. The silence in the dormitory grew tense, thick, unbearable. And then a smile of contempt spread slowly over my brother's face. "You fucking coward!" he finally said. He picked up a belt with a heavy buckle and began to approach the Jew, at first cautiously and then with more confidence. "Jewish son-of-a-bitch!"

In a corner of the dormitory, a few steps away, I watched the scene in slow motion, through eyes that had lost all sense of time and place. *Jewish traitor. Jewish murderer.* From the past came voices almost forgotten. They spilled from the attics that had long contained them into the oppressive silence of the dormitory. *Don't lie like a*

Jew. Don't spit on the floor like a Jew. Don't swear like a Jew. Only a Jew would betray his own brothers. Jewish traitor. Jewish cheat. Jewish thief. Jew. Jew.

My eyes finally moved, slid over the green bedspreads and stopped briefly, with fascination, on the trembling hand that held the pistol. And then I saw fear in the dark eyes, in the incredible paleness of the face.

"Shoot. I'm not afraid," my brother said. "That will be the day when a Jewish son-of-a-bitch scares me."

But the Jew wouldn't dare fire. His long, bony frame backed down steadily before Homero's defiant advance. *Half tender, half authoritative, a voice (was it my mother's?) admonished me: "Don't spit on the floor like a Jew."* The time came when the Jew could retreat no further. Homero kept advancing. The Jew looked at him with a mixture of hate and exhaustion. The faces of the other students in the dormitory had petrified. They were as still as the furniture and the walls.

And the silence grew overwhelming, broken only by Homero's slow, sure steps in search of his fate.

"THE OGRE!" someone shouted, destroying the tension. The silence was immediately broken by the noise of running feet. The normal activity had returned to the dormitory by the time Father Jorge entered and he noticed nothing. My brother, triumphant and admired, walked to the shower while the Jew collapsed on his bed, tired, defeated. I could not pry my eyes away from him. He returned my attention with a look devoid of light.

Later on, in the dark, several shadows fell over the Jew's bed; they held him, muzzled him, opened his wardrobe, took away his pistol and bullets, and gave him a taste of their fists just for the sake of it.

During the days that followed he stayed in bed, claiming to be sick. When he returned to class he desisted from talking, from paying attention to insults and practical jokes. In the long run his torturers started to forget about him. But he did not seem aware even of that: He lived like a phantom, or rather, as if the world were barely there. Sometimes, before the lights went out, I observed him flattened on his bed, crushed by the weight of a loneliness so great that it made me shudder. The pride I had felt for Homero would then dissolve into shame.

Hate, shame, rage. Years later I try in vain to regain them. To be furious, at least furious. Sheer rage to warm me up under these blankets that scarcely protect me from the Bogota cold, to make my blood boil, to melt this cover of ice that freezes my soul. But nothing happens. I feel nothing. And the young Jew vanishes once again with his pale face, with his black pistol, with his immense loneliness, with my hate, with my cruelty, with my shame...he vanishes, everything vanishes, and I am left dreaming that when I wake up tomorrow the warmth of emotion will be back in my life.

After my return from Cartagena it was not very difficult to improve my standing at school even more. In April I took first place, putting such a distance between Ruiz and me that my supremacy in the classroom seemed assured. The interclass soccer tournament had begun, and in spite of being so skinny and small, I had been included in my class' team, thanks mainly to my friendship with Iriarte, the captain. At the table my loquacity kept Ochoa at bay. Soon enough, I thought, I would overcome my condition of little boy, of "little angel," among my classmates.

My chats with Father Jorge had become regular and frequent. I no longer talked to him about my doubts, for by the plain device of closing my mind and ignoring them, they seemed to have disappeared. Our conversation had shifted from metaphysics to adulation: Father Jorge flattered me; I listened with great modesty and pleasure. Thus I learned, for example, that many other students, including some I scarcely knew, admired me greatly. Soon enough I began to consider myself the most virtuous person in the whole school.

The fact that I was not only a "virgin" but had preserved my body from the "solitary sin" was a source of immense pride for me. I acquired the pastime of trying to tell the "pure" from the "impure." In class, in the dormitory, in study hall, I analyzed personalities and distributed my verdict of guilt or innocence. At the top of the "impure" list I placed Ochoa, followed by—what a coincidence!—all those who for one reason or another I didn't like. Ochoa was not only corrupt but a hypocrite, as I would confirm every time he took communion, which happened every day. I felt pity for others because, though basically "good," they lacked willpower. I suspected that Homero should be counted among these, although I didn't really know why.

One night, after coming out of Father Jorge's room someone asked me when I was leaving for the seminary. Me? To the seminary? Me, who felt so uncomfortable about the sacraments? Me, who couldn't even think about the existence of God without doubting it? Ridiculous! I began to understand insinuations and jokes whose ironic sense had escaped me until that moment. They believed that Father Jorge was trying to talk me into becoming a priest! What else did they believe about my visits to Father Jorge's room? When was I leaving for the seminary? Father Jorge's hands moved all over my body with great freedom. More jokes, more insinuations. I felt myself blush suddenly, violently. I went to bed very disturbed. I would have to stop seeing Father Jorge. By morning, however, I had firmly decided not to surrender the "development of my personality" to the whims of "what other people might say."

At the beginning of May I began to feel weak and exhausted. A low but constant fever reduced me to a state of drowsiness. Father Jorge made me go to bed and called the doctor. The doctor ordered me to stay in bed two weeks. Two weeks! I couldn't remain away from class that long. But Father Jorge indicated curtly that I did not have any choice in the matter. Half an hour later two maids pushed in a cart with my lunch, and between the main course and dessert I resigned myself.

I spent most of my time sleeping, yawning useless thoughts, or fearing that Ruiz would take advantage of the situation to grab first place away from me.

A couple of days later, however, the Jew had one of his frequent illnesses—which no one took seriously—and I found myself with company. At first his presence three beds away annoyed me, I would rather be by myself. He did not seem anxious to talk to me either.

The following morning I heard a sob. The Jew was crying, his back turned to me.

"What's the matter with you? Do you want me to call somebody?"

Since he did not answer I got up and went to him. I sat on the next bed and tapped him on the shoulder: "Listen, what's the matter with you?"

He turned around, as if awakening. He fixed his eyes on me: "What do you want? Why did you wake me up?"

"I thought something was the matter with you."

"What do you mean? What could be the matter with me?"

"I heard you cry."

"Cry? Cry? Why in hell would I want to cry in front of you?"

"Well, excuse me, it isn't as if I were looking for a fight." I went back to my bed.

"Me crying?" he went on, "Don't give me that shit, you big-balled moron. And don't ever wake me up again, do you understand?"

He kept on insulting me for a while, until my patience was exhausted.

"Look," I told him, "you're sick, I'm sick, why make our lives more miserable? I got up because I thought you needed help. If I made a mistake I'm sorry. What else do you want me to tell you?"

He shut up.

"Where are you from?" I asked him later.

"That's none of your...from Cucuta. Your parents live in Cartagena, don't they?"

"Yes, have you ever been there?"

"Last year, with my family. Very pretty."

"What does your father do?"

"He owns a couple of drugstores. Yours is an engineer, isn't he?"

"Yes. A chemical engineer."

"Is that right? That's what I want to be when I grow up. Either that or an astronautical engineer."

"How come?"

"Rockets. I like rockets."

The conversation began to interest me a lot. "What kind of rockets?"

"All kinds. I believe that men will explore the moon and the planets. With big rockets. That's what I would like to do."

"Can you get that kind of work here in Colombia?"

"No. I'll have to go to the United States, if they ever get their rockets to work. Or else to Russia."

"But the Russians are Communists."

"I don't care as long as they let me work in their space program."

"And how do you know you will be any good at it?"

"Because I've already built several—small ones."

"Have you really? Do they fly?"

"A few I've built have gone up as high as three hundred meters. The problem is that they get damaged on landing, even though I install a small parachute on them."

Once he began to talk he couldn't hold back. With great enthusiasm he described the construction of his rockets and told me about his life in Cucuta, about his parents, and about his hero: his oldest brother, who was majoring in engineering in the United States and had taught him everything he knew about rockets. After being ostracized for so long his words flowed by the thousands, tripped over one another, fought to fill my ears. At home they called him Jaqui (his name was Jacobo Diaz), he loved to drink *curuba sorbete*, had once fallen from a horse and broken a leg, had been in Caracas, wanted to visit his brother in the United States.... We talked, or rather he talked, for hours and hours, until he exhausted himself into sleep after dinner.

When the other students returned he woke up and made a sign of greeting that I half answered. He seemed to be in high spirits. I forgot about him because Iriarte came and because Homero had a few things to discuss with me. When I looked at him again he had changed completely: his expression was one of near panic. Little by little I realized what was happening: he feared that I would betray his confidence, that I would expose him to ridicule. On his face grew the agonizing anticipation of jokes about

Jewish rockets and fetuses in orbit. I wanted to tell him something reassuring, but I didn't dare in front of Homero and the others. I smiled at him but he interpreted my smile as mockery, the first mocking smile of what was about to begin.

The following day he did little but sleep—or at least pretended to sleep. Since no one said anything to him that evening either, he must have felt relieved, for the next morning he got up a bit talkative, though still showing great mistrust. That afternoon Father Jorge sent him back to class and the monotony returned to the dormitory.

During the second week Father Jorge began to come around in the afternoon and that lessened my despairing boredom. "How is the patient this afternoon?" he would greet me.

"Ready to go back to class," I would answer, hoping that he would respond affirmatively. But he would just shake his head and sit next to my bed.

The inactivity brought many inconvenient "filthy thoughts" to my mind. I would fight them successfully while awake, but as soon as I sank into sleep they took complete control of me. I would often see myself as a gallant knight rescuing beautiful girls who would later give me their virginal bodies in gratitude. But other times my dreams would break all restraints. In one of them I had a nude girl asphyxiating inside a block of unprocessed sugar that deprived her of all movement. Just a moment before she would die I would break the block and revive her by licking the sweetness that covered her entire body. Once she was revived I would exercise my "rights" by entering her from the front and then from behind. After having satiated myself I would put her into another block of unprocessed sugar, her anguished pleas for pity not-

withstanding. Her suffering filled me with sexual pleasure until she was near suffocation. At that moment I
would break open the block and the scene would be repeated.

One afternoon when one such dream was delight-
ing—or torturing—me, a voice brought me back to the
luminous world of the awake.

"How is the patient this afternoon?"

"Fine," I answered Father Jorge, fearing that he
had realized what was going on.

"Forgive me," he added when he noticed my eyes'
effort to adapt to the light, "I didn't realize that you were
asleep."

"Don't worry, Father, it's the best thing that could
have happened."

There was an annoying silence between us. I could
swear that he was reading my mind. To end the increasingly unbearable situation I spoke, "Father, I want to
confess."

"Right now?"

"Yes, Father."

"With me?"

"Yes, Father."

"But are you ready?"

"Give me a few minutes and I will be."

I directed my eyes toward the green wall but it
reflected my gaze, which ended up finally on one of the
light bulbs on the ceiling. I tried to concentrate on the
prayers my lips murmured but my mind got lost in the
contemplation of the light bulb.

I finally turned my attention back to Father Jorge.
"Father, during the last few days I've been having a lot of
sickening dreams in which I do a lot of impure things."
Father Jorge raised his eyebrows, as if preparing for a long

story, but after a while he realized that I was not going to say anything more.

"Is that all?" he asked me.

"Yes, Father, but isn't that enough?"

"Boy, what you have just told me is not a sin."

"It isn't?"

"No. What one imagines when dreaming is not one's fault. It's impossible to have control over our dreams."

"Is that so?" I asked in surprise. "But, Father Jorge, if I dream 'filthy thoughts' it is because they are inside me. Isn't that right? Consequently it is my fault, isn't it?"

"No, Oscar, no. If it were your fault I would tell you."

"Father, I want to know about the solitary sin."

Father Jorge looked at me carefully, "Perhaps I will tell you tomorrow morning. Now I must go. See you," he said, patting me softly.

The morning came but he didn't. I forgot my frustration thanks to Iriarte's visit in the evening. He told me that Perez had beaten up Ruiz, to the applause of the rest of the class. He also told me that someone put a tack on Piggy's chair. The little man almost cried, more from outrage than from pain. Piggy called Pancho and, as a result, the whole class would be punished the following Saturday. (The punishment consisted of two continuous hours of standing at attention. Most of the students of secondary who were punished were there courtesy of Piggy, and spent the afternoon thinking about him.)

The following day Father Jorge let me go back to class on the condition that I would not try to play soccer during recess.

My classmates gave me a great reception. In their own fashion. In other words, they knocked on my head, wrote "little angel" in gigantic letters on the blackboard, and teased me as much as they could.

When I found out how much material they had covered during the preceding two weeks I despaired; it seemed nearly impossible for me to catch up. The teachers agreed to give me some extra time and that calmed my anxiety a little. After three days I felt able to take some of the exams, but after doing badly in the philosophy exam I decided to wait a bit longer. That very afternoon, however, I had a relapse and was forced to return to bed again. This time it would be a week, the doctor said. Every time I thought about Ruiz and the first place he was going to take away from me I felt terribly upset.

Three days after my return to bed one of Father Jorge's visits was becoming dull when he suddenly asked me, "Do you really want to know?"

"Want to know what, Father?"

"What masturbation is."

"Yes, Father."

"Well, it is the act of obtaining sexual pleasure through the auto-manipulation of the genital organ."

"Auto-manipulation?"

Father Jorge swallowed hard but continued with his explanation. "Exerting pressure with the hand, or stroking it, moving it until the satisfaction of the sexual urge."

I felt as if someone had kicked me in the face. That was the solitary sin? I had been doing it for five years now! I had always called it "having filthy thoughts." I recognized the sin in the enjoyment derived from the impure images. The part of the hands was always without importance, a secondary and mechanical event that accompanied the "filthy thoughts." And my dreams of sanctity? They were lost. I, the admirable child, actually had half a decade of practice!

"What's the matter with you?" Father Jorge inquired with alarm. On the verge of tears, I told him of my discovery and he, too, felt crushed. We remained silent, he looking at the floor and I at the ceiling. He was the first one to speak, after a long while.

"Are you sure?"

I looked at him without answering. Poor Father Jorge, I thought, he is as disappointed as I. My great virtue was nothing but ignorance of the terminology.

"Perhaps you didn't understand me correctly," he added, but his eyes indicated how small his hope was. No, Father, I thought, there is no way out.

I spoke at last, "According to what you told me, Father, I have been sinning for five years and hadn't even realized it."

"But you said that it was something secondary. Tell me, have you ever had an ejaculation while stroking your organ?"

"Ejaculation?"

"You don't know what an ejaculation is?"

"I don't know what the word means."

"Boy. The man's sperm is expelled at the moment of orgasm."

"Orgasm?"

"Sexual ecstasy," Father Jorge said, almost in despair.

"Oh, that," said I.

"Well?" Father Jorge charged again.

"No, I've never had one of those things," I said, scratching my head.

"Never?" Father Jorge's voice sounded excited. "And tell me, when you finished your filthy thoughts, did the organ remain hard or did it soften?"

"Hm, let me see, I think it remained hard. Yes, hard."

"Then you haven't committed it yet!" Father Jorge was triumphant.

"No?" I was surprised.

"No. You only had the beginnings of masturbation but without ever completing it. Besides, you didn't know it was a sin." He stood up and bid me goodbye, saying "Don't worry." He left the dormitory with a satisfied expression on his face.

I was not as relieved, however. Of course, I could not remember having had an ejaculation, but given the little attention I had paid to the matter, my sperm might have come out sometime without my noticing it.

How could I be such an idiot? How could I never have connected rubbing it with beating off? And I thought I was so alert and so intelligent! After hearing that kind of talk for years and years...I felt ashamed of my stupidity. No wonder Ochoa and the rest treated me as a little boy. A few hours earlier I was proud of my ignorance, it was the seal of my purity, now...a little boy, not a student of the fourth form of secondary, a baby...Ochoa and his smile of superiority! How could I face him now that I knew that after all we were of the same kind?

Dinner time finally came and I was able to forget about my problem. Or so I thought, for that night Homero brought news that made me begin the whole thing anew.

"You should have seen what happened in Piggy's class," he told me. "Duarte, you know him, the Fool Duarte, don't you? Well, the Fool Duarte was beating off in class and Piggy caught him. You should have seen how pissed off Piggy got. We all laughed so fucking hard! Well, he sent Duarte to stand by the blackboard. But the asshole was half asleep, you know. It seems he didn't even realize that he was in front of the class, or didn't care, because he went back to beating his meat just like that. Everybody broke up.

"Piggy finally noticed. You should have seen how pale he went. 'Degenerate! Degenerate!' he shouted. And then Perez, your classmate's brother, said aloud, 'Aw! Degenerate, bad boy!' And that's when it really began. I thought I was going to die. Piggy was practically crying. 'Corrupt! Shameless!' he yelled at us. At last he left. I thought that he went to get Pancho, but he didn't come back. I've never seen anything so funny."

That night the "solitary sin" plagued my dreams endlessly. In one of them I saw myself by the blackboard, rubbing my erect and naked penis in front of the class, while Piggy shouted "Degenerate! Degenerate!" at me. I wanted to stop but it was impossible, and I felt on the verge of tears. "Shame, shame!" Piggy yelled, and my classmates rolled on the floor unable to contain their laughter. In a corner, Ochoa repeated, "Once more and then communion, once more and then communion." From the door, Father Jorge urged me, "Don't let it soften, don't let it soften."

The following Monday I went back to class, this time for good. A few days later we received our grade books. I placed tenth, which was not too bad, considering that I had been absent most of the month and still lacked grades in several subjects. To my surprise, Iriarte and not Ruiz obtained first place. My detestable competitor was reduced to a modest fifth place.

After a few weeks the doctor let me play soccer again, and my return to class was thus complete. I made the assist for our only goal against fifth, and that made me happy even though we lost by an embarrassing score. About that time my favorite professional team, Millonarios, was fighting tenaciously for the lead of the tournament, a situation that led to feverish argument within our soccer circle. At last came the day of the Santa Fe-Millonarios game, in which Pinto had assured me Millonarios would be swept off the field. The opposite happened though, and when I didn't see him at school on Monday I figured that he had suddenly taken ill. He showed up on Tuesday to say that the referee had robbed Santa Fe of the game.

My sleep seemed to have become the playground for a series of masturbatory nightmares. Beat my cock, up, down, sideways. And the Guilt, Shame, the Little Boy Stupidity. I would wake up at midnight, tired from so much struggle, and immediately would touch myself to find out if anything was happening, if it had happened.

On a moonlit night a voice brought me out of my nightmare, "It's better to do that in the bathroom," the Jew told me. "That's where I am going right now," he added. He left. He had seen me. He had seen me! I thought of following him and explaining to him that I had been asleep, that I didn't do that kind of thing voluntarily. But I checked myself. How could I tell him that? No one would ever believe me.

From then on every time we met he winked at me. And at night, every night, while passing by my bed on his way to the bathroom he would greet me with a cheerful gesture. On his way back he would flash a victory sign. I wouldn't dare go to sleep until I could hear his soft, remote snoring. I did not want him to catch me in the act again. And in the early morning I would awaken before everyone else to prevent my damn dreams from exposing me.

The Jew had taken on a new life: He talked with his classmates, put up with their teasing, even told jokes. His former torturers didn't trust him but didn't reject him completely either. It was as if my masturbation had liberated him. He greeted me with great joy, with conspiratorial joy. And I didn't know what to do. I didn't dare insult him, on the one hand because it would be unfair after all he had suffered, on the other hand because I was afraid that he might tell on me. I could already hear the mockery: "Little Angel beats his meat."

Whenever I saw him happy among those who used to hate him I would shiver with wrath. It was a lie, Goddamnit! I had not done it on purpose, I had been asleep. When anyone from the Jew's class as much as hinted a smile at me I suspected sarcasm. And then I would be even more upset. Why should his happiness depend on my being ridiculed, Goddamnit!

He grew friendlier toward me every day. So I cannot really understand why I did it. Very casually, as an afterthought, I told Becerra, a bastard from our dormitory, about the Jew's nocturnal activities. "The Fetus? Does he? That fucking Fetus!" And the son-of-a-bitch, Becerra, started to laugh. For a while afterwards I dreaded that he might tell the Jew because they might have become friends, or just to hurt me or to hurt us both. My fears were in vain: One could always count on Becerra for the worst.

That night I saw the Jew go to the bathroom happier than usual. About a minute later I heard whispers, quiet laughs, and the bare steps of Becerra and three other toughs on their way to the bathroom. My ear lost track of them but I imagined them in the dark bathroom, tiptoeing toward the cubicle where they could half glimpse the Jew's legs with pajamas hanging around his ankles.

Suddenly, like lightning, the bathroom light came on.

"Ha, ha, ha," came the laughs. "Look at that cut-up cock!"

"Ha, ha."

"It's none of your business."

"Looks like spaghetti."

"More like the umbilical cord of an aborted fetus."

"Bunch of sons-of-bitches."

There was the sound of scuffling and a crash against the wall.

"Motherfucking Jew! Jewish son-of-a-bitch!"

"Ouch!"

"Ha, ha. Don't let him put his pants back on!"

"Sons-of-bitches, if you like to look so much, look! I am going to do it on you!"

"You fucking Jew!"

At that moment Father Jorge's voice was heard, "What's happening here? For God's sake! What do you all think you're doing?"

"The Jew was beating off, Father."

"Yes, Father, we figured as much and caught him."

"What? Is that true, Diaz? Diaz, what do you think you are doing, you miserable...? How dare you?"

The crack of a slap on the face echoed through the dormitory.

There was weeping. "How dare you hit me, you queer priest? Yes! Queer! QUEER!"

Another slap on the face.

"FAGGOT!"

Sound of struggle.

"OUCH! Let me go! Fucking priest."

Fists.

"Miserable Jew...motherfucker...you don't talk to a priest like that."

"Let him go," Father Jorge said.

"Father, we can't let him insult our religion."

"That's right, Father."

"We have to teach him that we Catholics know how to defend ourselves."

"Let me go! Motherfuckers! Let me go!"

"Understand me well," Father Jorge spoke to him, barely containing himself. "Tomorrow you will leave this school. We have shown extraordinary patience. But enough is enough. We don't want to see you around here again. Never."

"What else could I ask for? Bunch of bastards and queers."

They left him in the bathroom, crying and swearing. Father Jorge warned us—by then we were all very wide awake—that he did not want to hear a single word out of us for the rest of the night. "And be careful not to touch even one hair on Diaz' head. He won't be here tomorrow."

The Jew took an eternity in returning to the dormitory. I couldn't sleep. I felt it had been my fault. And I was afraid of his revenge. Of his telling, shouting, that I masturbated. "Little Angel also beats his meat!" Or of his beating me up for being a fink. At worst he would have another revolver hidden somewhere. But when he returned to his bed he did not make the slightest noise. The next day he went away forever.

Toward the end of June we played our last soccer game against the other section of fourth, the surprising leader of the tournament. After losing all the other games we were hoping for a victory over the virtual champions. Not only did we lose miserably but at dinner Iriarte and I had to put up with teasing from Duran, our other table mate, who had scored three goals for the winners.

"Goddamnit," Iriarte said. "Only when they join the two sections next year will I be able to win a fucking game."

My relationship with Father Jorge suffered some-what: We now avoided chastity and other hitherto favorite topics to the point that we often did not know what to talk about. With time I went to his room less and less. One day he complained, but I told him that because of my illness I was way behind in my studies and had to spend a lot of time catching up.

That was a lie, of course, and he probably knew it. My schoolwork was actually becoming easier every day. The slightest effort enabled me to perform like a virtuoso in any class. Even Pancho and the Rector, who taught us world literature, were impressed. But my major accomplishment was to secure the highest grade in geometry. Professor Reyes hated boys of tender age who obtained good grades in other classes, for he thought they were the Escolapians' pets. To show how fair he was to everyone, he made the poor pets' lives miserable. He must have convinced himself that I was different. Only in draftsmanship and the subjects that Piggy allegedly taught did I have to rub elbows with my classmates.

Even though I tried to appear modest, my vanity knew no limits. My sense of security and superiority was total—few were the things I did not believe myself capable of doing. The world was mine in those days and I treated it with the arrogance I employed toward servants.

As the semester exams approached, the students' war against Piggy grew in intensity. He was responsible for the punishment of ever increasing numbers every Saturday. We began to get even on the following Mondays. And no revenge surpassed the caricatures that showed him as a big-headed piglet. Piggy found them pinned to the blackboard, in his desk, and even inside his briefcase. His ire fed on itself as it grew. The caricatures were drawn by Carlos Miller, one of my classmates and soon to become one of my closest friends. It was Piggy's great fortune to catch Carlos' brother, Rodrigo, putting one of the drawings in the chalk box. Since Rodrigo refused to identify the artist, Pancho expelled him.

In the days that followed there were more expulsions in what looked like a desperate effort to save Piggy. Representatives from all the classes met on the sly and agreed on a plan to get rid of the hated instructor. Our class would be the first to put it into effect.

On the morning of the chosen day Piggy found the class in complete silence. With a suspicion of triumph in his eyes he began to call roll. No one answered. He called Iriarte and others to the blackboard and they went but did not utter a word. Piggy soon lost control and told us with great color and energy his opinion of us and our future, and compared us with rather disagreeable characters from shameful episodes of ancient times and from the police pages of contemporary newspapers. We remained mute, however, and the little man decided to change tactics.

Piggy called me and I went up front. "Moreira, I know that you are a responsible person who is not intimidated by others, aren't you."

Silence.

"Or are you going to tell me that the toughs in this class frighten you?"

Silence.

"How can it be possible for the best student in this class, the best in the whole school, to behave in this manner?"

I hesitated and Piggy noticed the impact of his flattery.

"That's right, the best student in the whole school should set an example, particularly when his classmates don't know how to behave." I felt the group's alarm.

Piggy smiled. "Read this paragraph, here, the first one," he said, showing me the open book.

But I stepped back, away from him, and in my eyes he saw the defiance of the entire class. Silence. He had lost.

Pancho was quick to punish us. But to no avail. The same thing happened in all the other classes. The following day we found out that Piggy had resigned, though another version suggested that he had been fired.

Every time we received gradebooks I placed first comfortably. And in the mid-year exams I gained an enormous margin over any possible competitors. I began to think that the honor sash would be mine at the end of the year. This time when the plane home took off from Bogota I looked at the city below with fondness. Even the sun bestowed its mighty light on the beautiful forest of red-tiled roofs that grew smaller and smaller. I felt master of my own fate and completely happy.

4

The month-long midyear vacation in Cartagena had been all I had anticipated, and thus I returned to El Calasanz refreshed and eager. But the great future that I seemed to have before me was not to be. It all began rather innocently, with a letter from my mother mentioning that the family might have to move to Bogota. Her remark read as an afterthought, but it caused so much anxiety in me that I could no longer concentrate on my studies. Life was just as I wished it to be; that sort of change could not be for the best. Nor did I think it was merely a possibility. No, her off-the-cuff tone was just her way of smoothing the path for the bad news coming our way. And sure enough, a week later another letter came to tell us that the board of directors had declared the petrochemical company bankrupt. A government bureaucrat, totally ignorant of the company's existence, had signed contracts for the importation of enough petrochemical products to supply all of the country's needs for several years. When the company found out, it was too late: There were no markets left, no prospects; liquidation was the only choice. My father would look for a job or establish his own business once in Bogota.

My father came to Bogota and took us house hunting during the weekend. We expected to look in some of the better neighborhoods like El Chico, or Santa Ana, where we had owned a home just a few months earlier. It was a beautiful house in the woods, with a panoramic view of the city. It was my parents' dream house, built to their specifications. But shortly before we could move in, my father accepted the job in Cartagena and the house went on the market. Homero and I thought it was a shame to have sold that house only to end up moving to Bogota.

My father gave us an unpleasant surprise, however. "We can't buy a comparable house because this move wasn't planned and I may need to invest my capital," he said. So instead of El Chico or Santa Ana we went to El Polo Club, a middle-class neighborhood not too far from El Calasanz. We looked at tract housing, two-story duplexes with brick facades and large windowpanes. The duplexes were new, some not yet finished, and reminded us of the company houses where we had spent the greater part of our lives. It was the last day of sunshine before the rainy season, and the blue sky, the warm light, and the smell of fresh paint gave me a comforting feeling of familiarity. The move was a big letdown after Cartagena, but perhaps it wouldn't be too bad. Thus I took my father's choice of a house in El Polo Club in my stride; but my spirit of sacrifice weakened considerably as the day approached when I would leave the boarding section to become a commuter. Dark forebodings about my family's financial situation and a myriad of other things crossed my mind until there was no longer room in it for school work and my other normal concerns. I can't go on like this, I said to myself. This is absurd. And I often thought of running to Father Jorge, of letting him be once again guardian of my dreams and my protector against silly mirages and threatening realities. But something in me had changed; I had pulled away, I had built a barrier between us. And so when I was packed and came to his room all I could muster was a "Thank you for everything, Father."

"We are going to miss you in the boarding section," he said. And then as I left, he added: "Everything will be alright, Oscar. God goes with you."

My father drove us to the houses we had visited,
went to the end of the street and turned right, leaving us
perplexed. We found ourselves in a previously unnoticed
jungle of two-story buildings made of concrete. I soon
realized that they were houses, hundreds of ugly houses
glued to one another and completely alike in their gray
and white monotony.

The greatest fear took hold of me. This could not
be, we were not going to live here, were we? But the car
unmercifully rolled to a stop at a corner and I could not
escape the fact that such a place was my new home.

It was a gray, gray, gray house, so gray that not
even the occasional white patches and bare bricks of the
facade were noticeable. A few sprouts of wild grass here
and there, a chunk of construction debris farther away, a
piece of cold, naked soil nearby indicated that the house
had been born poor in atmosphere and rich in ugliness.

Two stories rose above the ground; the first one
began timidly behind the garage (which resembled a jail
because of its high iron fence). The second one provided
the roof for the garage and exposed a balcony and a small
window to the street. We went into the dark living room
where in the midst of furniture in absolute disarray, my
mother, Dora, and the baby stood waiting for us. My
mother was so excited that she did not notice my disappointment. "What happiness!" She said, "Imagine, a house
of my own, all my own. At last, after so many years. Thank
God." From the living room we could see the backyard,
not a large one. Circling through it we found the servants'
room and then the kitchen, which offered doors to the
dining room and bar. After the bar came the living room

again.

On the second floor a large room looked onto the street through the small window I had seen earlier. The door to the small balcony on the corner funneled the Bogota cold into the room whenever opened. That would be my parents' bedroom. Three other bedrooms, small ones, took up most of the remaining space. "One for Dora, one for the baby, and one for the two boys," as my father told my mother. Two minute bathrooms with skylights made of plain glass completed that section of the house. The house had everything, but everything it had was ugly.

Homero and I entered our bedroom, whose only window faced the backyard. Homero sat on one of the cots. (Since we had always lived in company housing, our own furniture was minimal.) "Father says that they are going to buy us a bedroom set as soon as they can," he said. I tried to find in him some sign of disappointment to match mine, but he seemed completely indifferent.

Through the window I noticed that the color of the sky was the same I ascribed to the house: leaden. The clouds thickened slowly, lazily, growing in blackness as well as in density.

I went down to the dining room, thinking that I could be alone there. The large window pane would have made for a bright room elsewhere, but there only a soft twilight filtered down from the cloudy Bogota sky.

One, two, three, four drops of water tapped on the glass and began to slide down slowly. In a few seconds the rhythm of the tapping increased and then stabilized as rain. I touched the glass with my forehead and found it cool and fresh. All the houses across the street were identical to ours. I felt ashamed of being there, of having to call home the nightmare of symmetry that surrounded me. A furtive tear slipped down my cheek just as my mother walked into the room.

"Instead of standing there making yourself miserable, you should be upstairs helping Homero," she said coldly.

"Yes, Mother."

When I was crossing the threshold she added, "Thank God for what He has given you. Don't be an ingrate."

Upstairs I found Homero fixing up the room. "This side of the closet for you; I'll take the other."

"Aha."

"The bed in the corner is mine."

"The cot?"

"Whatever."

"What do you mean yours?"

"I asked for it first."'

"So what? I'm the oldest."

"The oldest! Big deal! Look, stupid asshole, if you want the corner you'll have to take it away from me."

At that moment my father came into the room. When he left, the cot in the corner was mine. Homero was obviously displeased. To upset him even more I made faces at him until he went out, swearing at me.

I was beginning to hang my clothes when he returned with a box and a piece of cloth.

"What is that?" I asked him.

"A box and a piece of cloth."

"Of course, it takes an asshole not to know that."

"Why did you ask then?"

"Damnit, what is it for?"

"To put your radio on top," he answered, blushing first and then smiling, though his smile was tight, as if it took effort for him to admit that he could be a nice person.

I returned his smile, minus the grimace, and took

the radio out of its box. Did Homero feel as I did?

Bogota is the place in the world where the sun never sets; it simply disappears behind the mountains when you are least aware. Suddenly the night falls upon you and you know that the day has ended. We were just beginning to unpack when we were called to supper.

That first Monday as a commuter I felt out of place in El Calasanz. My routines, my timing were those of a boarder. I saw Iriarte, Ochoa, Duran and my other former fellow boarders file out of the dormitory on their way to class, and I wished that I could join them. But I no longer belonged with them. I was now an outsider. Ruiz hurried to greet me that morning—a rare event. My move to El Polo Club must have given him great satisfaction.

At the end of the day Homero and I left on foot with Carlos Miller, my classmate, and his brother Rodrigo (who returned to school when Piggy left). We walked five blocks through La Castellana, El Calasanz's neighborhood, and then through a grassy field; we jumped over a stream of dirty water, crossed the railroad line, and found ourselves in El Polo. From that point it was three blocks to the Miller's home, which faced a small square, and two more blocks to ours. Since there were few houses in La Castellana, and thus little traffic, we took to playing soccer on our way home from school: two against two, whoever got to the grassy field with the ball won.

I liked the Millers but I did not care much for their friends. Rodrigo's girlfriend was allegedly very beautiful, but I found her rather plain. After a few weeks I came to the conclusion that there was not a single attractive girl in the whole neighborhood. As a consequence, every time we were invited to parties I would decline. Homero always went. "But why don't you go? You'll have a good time, meet pretty girls, maybe find a girlfriend," my mother would tell me.

"No, I don't feel like it, they are all ugly, I have to study."

There was something about the people of the neighborhood that I hated. I could not say for sure what it was, however. Perhaps it was the sticky accent—"grimy," as my mother called it. "*Ala*, but what a tremendous thing, how could you even think it, *alita*?" Damned Bogotanians. *Rolos*. "So shremendous." And the conversation about clothes, and "Miami," and "How could you even think it, alita?" About horse races, and-the Imperio "theasher" on 63rd Street where they could see French movies in spite of being underage. And the trips to bars, dark and filthy lairs, to play billiards and drink beer in the afternoon, when they should be in school.

And the talk about the "old ladies, *ala*." "A divine woman, I just have to introduce her to you," and you knew that she was uglier than a fart, as they all were, either fat or bony—never just slender—shapeless, feeble, with pink cheeks. "*Ala*, but how well you look." Short. Nothing like the girls from Caldas, or the ones from Cartagena. No, lifeless, driveling morons. Damned *Rolos*. And I detested them. Join their circle? To live among them was repugnant enough. Homero suggested that I was too conceited and we had words.

It felt strange having my father around the house in the daytime during the week. He got up early, as was his habit, bombarded us with questions during breakfast and watched us depart. Some days he would drive away in his car to follow a lead for a job or a business. But much of the time he waited at home for someone to call him back, to send him a contract in the mail. He was not used to waiting and thus became more nervous and irritable each day, more uncertain of himself. He had always had a job, a definite plan of action. As the situation dragged on for weeks and weeks he began to panic, to the point that he decided to go back to church every Sunday, something I had never seen him do.

For a couple of weeks he entertained the idea of moving to the United States. He brought home information about housing, schools, and so on, and talked to us about it with great enthusiasm. It would be best to move to a small city, like Sacramento in California, where the climate was not too cold in the winter. Homero and I grew very excited about the prospective move, especially after we read in a high school bulletin that courses in astronomy were offered.

Unfortunately, one of my father's ideas for a business materialized. He had been trying to buy the rights to a distributing house for petrochemical products, thinking that it would be only fair to participate in the bonanza produced by the events that had cost him his position in Cartagena. According to the information he had—two friends from college were involved in similar businesses—it produced more money than a parish. He was suddenly notified of an opening. The paperwork would take about two months and we would have to invest most of our money. My father was obviously relieved, and our life in Bogota began to take on a sense of normalcy. My parents bought furniture, draperies, and various other accessories for the house. And one day my father came home in a brand new station wagon.

I would have preferred the move to the United States, but even so, the end of my father's uncertainty signaled the end of mine as well. Until then my waking hours had seemed to disappear in the half-lighted corners, curves, and turns of the house. From my arrival after school till my bedtime I did little but pace about, as if looking in the walls for answers to questions I could not even formulate. My school work suffered, I lost ground, even went to exams unprepared. I exhorted myself, came home determined to work, but once in the house my intellectual torpor would make me incapable of action. Still, I thought that things would take care of themselves while I managed to overcome my perplexing, senseless musing. Thus the first time we received grade books I was shocked to learn that I had lost my first place to Iriarte. I was gracious enough to congratulate my friend, and now rival, but I felt that an abyss had been carved between the world and me. I could see my classmates' faces but now they seemed to belong to strangers, and I could see the desks, the blackboard, the door, the windows, but they no longer had that familiar air that bound me to the very buildings of the school.

As in a dream, I played soccer with the Millers on the way home. As in a dream, I casually told my mother that I had placed third. As in a dream, I sat on my bed to listen to the radio. As in a dream, I saw Homero leave the room and close the door. But then I wept very real tears for what had been mine.

Never again, I promised myself. Nevertheless, the next month I worked no harder. Indeed, for the first time in my life I failed an exam. After answering two questions in geometry with some difficulty, my mind went blank. The paper drifted away from me, the lines blurred, a cold sweat dampened my brow.

"What's the matter with you? Why don't you write?" Professor Reyes' voice.

"I feel ill."

"You chose the worst moment to feel ill. Better hurry up because there isn't much time left."

I returned to the exam. Nothing. I could think of nothing. I stood up and handed the exam to Professor Reyes. "I feel very ill. I can't continue." He took my paper and shrugged his shoulders.

On Monday I asked him to give me another chance to take the exam. He refused at first, but after I swore and swore again that I had been ill he consented to give me an oral exam. It was then that my father's business idea came through and my mind was again capable of sustained effort. I prepared conscientiously for that second exam, and I thought I did very well in it.

During all this time I was surprised to see how little the situation seemed to affect my mother. Perhaps living in a house all her own was immensely satisfying. She truly enjoyed taking care of the baby, arranging the furniture, giving orders to the maid, a cranky old woman. But more than anything, my mother relished doing the housework herself. She would put on old clothes and begin swinging a mean broom all over her new house; she would then buff and shine the wooden floors, wash windows crystal clear, polish metal ornaments and leave the china spotless. It was a labor of love. The maid was there mostly for cooking. Didn't my mother miss Cartagena? Didn't she wish we had never sold the house in Santa Ana? But she went on cleaning and running the house, all the while singing, smiling, or laughing at her own teasing.

She appeared to be annoyed only by the door-to-door salesmen who interrupted her work, although it is fair to say that they were at a terrible disadvantage. My mother would open the door, and before the salesman could open his mouth she would say something like

"Juanita is not home. Go away."

"What? What do you mean?"

"Listen, you already got her pregnant. What else do you want? If you aren't going to take responsability, why don't you leave her alone?"

After an opening like that it was very unlikely that he would even try to peddle his wares. He would extricate himself as best he could and make sure he never stopped at that address again. He should count his blessings, though. When my mother would see a salesman making his way from house to house down the street, she would don her special just-arrived-from-the-hills, dumb-maid costume, complete with soot smeared on her face and bare feet. Broom in hand, she would answer the door.

"Is the lady of the house in?"

"Whatcha mean is th' lady of th' house in?" my mother answered with a most pronounced hill accent. It was obviously an imitation but the salesmen never caught on.

"Yes, the lady, if you would, please."

"No, 'Oly Mother Mary! God ain' goin' tuh let me do that."

"But what's wrong with asking for the lady?"

"Watcha mean what's wrong? Yuh rotten bum. Th' husbin' leave fo' work an' yuh come tuh git th' wife. Virgin uh Chiquimquira! These people ain' got no respect no how, not even fo' th' Lord hisself."

"Look here. I'm just trying to make a living."

"But ain' it too much? Pure Mother Mary! What a shameless bum! He's got tuh git paid on top uh it!"

The salesmen were not the only ones who disapproved of such behavior. A house guest once remarked privately to me that he was fully sympathetic to my "situation" (meaning my strange mother). "Oh, yes," I said. "You can't imagine how trying it can be. But you will get a better idea soon. She is planning a big surprise for you tomorrow."

Among those who had been amused by her antics with the salesmen were three brothers who lived two doors down from us. We had seen them walking by many times, but did not speak to them until the time when Homero and I were playing soccer outside and a ball that bounced the wrong way hit one of the brothers in the head.

"Damnit!" he yelled. "Can't you be careful?"

We came over to apologize.

"You should be more careful," he insisted.

"Aw, com'on," his oldest brother told him. "This wouldn't have happened if you knew how to head the ball properly."

The oldest brother then smiled at us. "I'm Alvaro Tellez," he said and then extended his hand. We smiled back and introduced ourselves. The other two brothers were named Benito and Ciro. Alvaro was a year older than I, and Ciro a year younger than Homero. Benito, the one with the bump on the head, was in between. Alvaro, Benito, and Ciro. The Tellez ABC.

They accepted immediately when we invited them to play on the street. We chose a couple of small, recently planted trees as the goal. Ciro served as goalie and the others played "21," the Moreiras against the Tellezes. At the end of an hour and a half the Tellezes won 21-19.

From then on we played very frequently, almost every afternoon, choosing sides at random. One day we went to Miller's Square (as we informally called it) and beat everybody. Five against five. Pavement and ball. Frightening pedestrians and competing with automobiles. Ruining shoes, and pants, and gardens, and saplings that would never grow. Goal! No, it wasn't. What do you mean it wasn't? Cheaters....

And then a bottle of soda pop with Carlos and Rodrigo Miller. "You guys must have been practicing together a lot," Carlos said.

My religious doubts had subsided only because I ignored them. But the apologetics class brought them to the surface time and again. I found St. Thomas Aquinas' arguments for the existence of God so unconvincing that I couldn't help fighting Father Miguel all the way.

"Father, you say that an infinite retrogressive series defies the laws of logic, that because of it there must be a first cause. But what can you tell me about numbers? Isn't that a counterexample? Negative numbers form an infinite retrogressive series. How come that doesn't defy the laws of logic?"

"Numbers are not things, Moreira."

"But so what, Father? The reason you gave was that infinite retrogressive series were illogical. You didn't specify that they had to be series of things."

"Look, you know I was referring to physical objects. Numbers are an exception."

"Why are they.an exception, Father?"

"It's very clear: numbers are something intellectual, physical objects are...physical."

"I don't understand why logic applies to some but not to the others."

"Don't you understand?"

"No, Father."

"Look, Moreira, if you want to understand you will have to study more." But the following day I would be undeterred.

"Father Miguel, you claim that because no object can put itself in motion there must be a prime mover. But why couldn't motion be the natural state of things?"

"Look, if you weren't a decent kid, I would say that you're trying to give me a hard time. What you say is ridiculous; it amounts to saying that there is something eternal besides God."

"But aren't you assuming precisely what we are trying to prove? And another thing, Father—"

"Moreira!"

It was in such a moment of frustration that Perez unearthed the passage from *Summa Contra Los Gentiles* in which St. Thomas argues that sibling incest is wrong because if the love between husband and wife is combined with that between brother and sister, the result is an excessive amount of sexual relations.

Father Miguel was terribly embarrassed. "You shouldn't pay attention to a minor aspect of St. Thomas' philosophy," he said.

That same day, as I was walking toward the soccer field, I saw Father Miguel talking to Father Jorge, who signaled to me to come over.

"Oscar," Father Jorge asked me, "why are you giving Father Miguel a hard time?"

Father Miguel smiled at me and I realized that he wasn't really complaining.

"I am not trying to make trouble for you, Father."

"I know. Actually, the point of the class is that people should be able to ask questions."

Father Jorge put his hand on my shoulder. "Oscar, what has happened to your school work?

I felt very uncomfortable. "I don't know, Father."

"Come on, Jorge," Father Miguel said. "Anyone needs time to adapt to this city."

There was more than normal interest behind Father Jorge's question. He probably knew already that I had placed seventh this time.

It must be a mistake, I told myself. I looked at the grade book carefully; in front of geometry there was a single number: 1. (The grades were on a scale from 0 to 5; 5 was the highest, 3 was passing.) It's a mistake. It has to be a mistake. During the following hour we had Professor Reyes' class. As soon as it ended I asked him what grade he had given me.

"The grade you earned."

"But, Professor, what grade is that?"

"What does the gradebook say?"

"One."

"Correct. It's a one."

"A one?" I felt very weak.

"With the exam you wrote, what did you expect?"

"But, Professor, what about the oral exam?"

"What about the oral exam? I wanted to see whether you could impress me enough to raise your grade. And I did raise it. From 0.5 to 1."

I was stunned. This could not be. It could not be. Pinto and Hoyos came over. The teacher left the room.

"He's not fair," Pinto said.

"What a dirty trick," Hoyos added.

Iriarte came over, too. He had placed first again. "I'm really sorry, Oscar."

"Thanks, man, thanks."

Later on I asked him to let me look at his grades. Mine were generally better. Had I received my normal grade in geometry I would have placed first.

Later that afternoon I took a bus to run an errand for my father. Through the bus window I saw the Bogota sky turn gray. Gray sky. Gray city. Huge and cold. It was unfair, very unfair. I deserved first place. The sky became black with a crash of thunder. Raindrops began to trace ditches in the dirt on the window. Unfair. I'm going to get wet. Unfair. That Reyes was a son-of-a-bitch. "Yes, I raised your grade. From 0.5 to 1." As if he had done me a great favor. Son-of-a-bitch. The window wouldn't close tight and the water began to drip on my head. Goddamn Bogota rain. Goddamn Bogota.

5

Things were finally settling down. I had to be patient. My father already had a business and might be on his way to becoming a millionaire.

But I was afraid. What if we could never get out of that pigsty of a house, of a neighborhood?

I should have more confidence. Eventually we would move to El Chico...or Santa Ana...or El Rosario.

And I would dream of mansions in the best neighborhoods of Bogota, of an eternity of first places. My mind would fill with light and warmth and would travel far from Bogota, to Cartagena, the Caribbean sun burning the stones of San Felipe...life in the breeze...paradise of palm trees...of water, of sea, of sky...true rain storms, manly storms, not like this cold, slithery...thing...drizzle...of Bogota that lasts hours and days and weeks. Or to the mountains of Caldas...true mountains...covered by coffee plantations. And I would dream about a future in El Chico, in Bocagrande, or about the past in Bocagrande, in Caldas...life in the breeze...and about her. One her, two, three, many...She...She. Lucia, in Pereira. Oh! Those big blue eyes, blinding eyes...that delicious mouth. Justina, my aunt's maid, in Bocagrande. Naked in the backyard...bright red hair against the guanabanas...and that skin so white against the trunk of the papaya tree...and my uncle Fabio taking his shirt off... *Come here, darling, come and I'll show you how much I love you*...and those breasts of hers that seemed to grow even bigger...and that dark-red pubic hair. And how she moved, her hips dancing against the trunk of the papaya tree...*Don Fabio! Oh! Don Fabio*...his shirt on the ground...*Come, dear, let's go into the bedroom*...My uncle's mouth kissed her, kissed her, seemed to suck her blood, her soul...Don Fabio... My uncle's fingers closing on her reddish pubic hair...*Let's hurry up, darling, let's go into the bedroom. Let's hurry up. Before they come back.*

My aunt Elena discussing with my mother, "Justina is such a good maid."

"Yes, dear, you are so lucky. And such a good looking peasant."

"Yes, at first people even think that she belongs to the family. Such poise."

Come, darling, let's hurry up.

"Of course. She has more going for her than many society people I know."

"That's true."

...*Don Fabio, Don Fabio*...

"Where did you get her?"

"In Santander, dear. Over there in Santander even the beggars have the look of decent people."

...The red hair against the green of the guanabana...and later, her hand caressing my hair...*what a cute boy*...and my face the color of her hair.

Back in my room in El Polo: the light blue walls that were gray instead, the ceiling of dull white, the two green bedspreads—the only note of color—the window...the leaden light that came through the window...She...Justina...white against the trunk of the papaya tree...red against the green of the guanabana...The temptation, the short struggle with myself...open the door, make sure there isn't anyone else upstairs...to the bathroom...close and lock the door, turn on the water for noise, just in case...down with the pants...Justina...*what a cute boy*...and Father Jorge...You are an exceptional boy...*Power and Purity*: "...they stop believing in God so as to excuse their bad conduct." Lord, help me...My hand freezes. I stand up, turn off the water. Back to my room...gray, horribly gray . . . it's going to rain...Goddamn town...She, but not Justina...I should be ashamed...a vulgar woman...a maid...yes, a maid..."I can forgive you anything except chasing maids...it's so filthy." Filthy...a maid...dreaming of a maid...shame...No. *She*, the true she...product of my dreams: beautiful, perfect...long blonde hair, big eyes like Lucia's, blue like Lucia's...but blonde hair...so elegant, always, as in a dream...and mine, all mine...give her a name...a goddess' name it must be...Diana or Venus...better Diana, like the hunter...blonde, with blue blinding eyes...product of my dreams...if you really exist...she has to exist...mine...Diana, my goddess and my slave...Homero comes in...my fantasies end.

Dora's eleventh birthday fell on a Sunday in the middle of October. Not on any Sunday, but precisely when Millonarios, the league leader, played against Medellin, in second place, in El Campin. The Tellezes, who possessed several courtesy passes, had invited me and I thought of nothing else all week. But on the day of the game my father announced that I had to join the family picnic in honor of Dora's birthday.

"But, Father. . ."

"Don't argue with me. It's the least you can do for your sister."

"But, Father, it's the game between Millos and Medellin!"

Suddenly he grabbed me by the shirt collar and picked me up: "Get ready to come with us! And straighten your face or I'll do it for you!"

I was as disturbed by his loss of control as I was upset over not being able to see the game. On the way back from the picnic I heard on the car radio that the game had ended in a tie—one to one. The result was actually favorable to Millonarios. But the following morning Hoyos and Pinto were claiming that even at home those clods of Millos couldn't handle a decent team like Medellin.

In November we began to prepare for the final exams. Carlos Miller suggested studying with Nieto, who was in danger of flunking. Alberto Nieto, though scarcely two years older than Carlos, looked at least twenty-one and was rumored to have been on the verge of marriage once. Not that he was too big; he was actually rather short and of average weight for his height, but he had an older face and a thick beard that he shaved every day. Next to him Carlos and I, both skinny and puberty-faced, looked like a couple of runts. Alberto also lived in El Polo but he traveled by school bus. By November he was flunking four subjects—three being enough to be held back. Since it was primarily for his benefit that we were going to study together, we decided to accept Alberto's offer to meet at his place. He was an only son and thus we could find in his house the peace and quiet we desired.

It turned out to be even quieter because his parents were vacationing on the coast. We had the house entirely to ourselves, except for the kitchen and the servant's room, which were occupied by the maid and her daughter.

The first night Carlos came by after dinner and we walked together to Alberto's house, two blocks away.

Alberto opened the door. "Come on in."

"Ready?" Carlos asked.

"One moment." He turned around and I realized that we had arrived in the middle of a conversation, for another person was standing in the living room. The figure moved out of the shadows and I found myself before the one beautiful girl I had seen in the neighborhood—slender body, nice breasts, long brown hair, big, clear eyes, perfect red mouth.

"The Coca-cola is in the refrigerator," she said to Alberto.

"Thank you."

She passed by Carlos and placed a foot outside the door. Carlos smiled at her and she half-returned his smile. "See you later," she said to Alberto.

"See you later," Alberto answered. She went out and closed the door.

"Huummnn, *mama mia,*" Carlos mumbled. "Alberto, what kind of friend are you? Why didn't you introduce us to your sister? I thought you were an only child."

"I am. She's not my sister; she's the maid's daughter."

"The maid's...?"

"The maid's daughter?"

"Yes."

"Man," Carlos told him, "we weren't trying to insult you."

"Don't worry, guys. It happens to everyone."

"What's her name?" Carlos asked.

"Rosario."

"Can I come to your house to spend my vacation?" kidded Carlos.

"Certainly, you're welcome to."

We went up to Alberto's room, which was the counterpart to mine in my house. The rear part of Alberto's house was different, though. Instead of the backyard under the window, his had the servant's quarters separate from the rest of the house. Alberto had a magnificent view of the maid's bathroom window.

"Hum, rather convenient, isn't it?" Carlos commented. "You can see the maid, and that terrific daughter of hers if they forget to close the curtain. I assume that you stay glued to the window."

"Sometimes they forget. What I do is turn the light off and open the Venetian blinds. That way I can look at them without their seeing me."

"How old is she?"

"Rosario? Fourteen."

"And have you tried to...?"

"No, as much as I would like to...no. if I fuck her I may ruin her life...she might have to stay a maid like her mother. Or I might have to marry her. As it is, her mother is sending her to school. And since she is pretty and looks like she belongs to a decent family she may have a future."

I finally said something. "Yes, it would be a rotten thing to do."

"Of course it would be a rotten thing to do," Carlos hurried to add, "but, at any rate...I think I would go crazy living here with pussy like that under the window."

"You're telling me," Alberto sighed. "Sometimes I think that I am going to explode." And changing the topic, "Well, fuckers, how about hitting the books?"

It was midnight when at last we finished studying for the French exam and left Alberto's house. Carlos walked me home.

"That's what I call a broad," he commented.

"Yes...but she's a maid."

"What a pity," he said.

From then on we went to Alberto's every night. After French we had English and then two days to study anatomy. We soon found ourselves studying until two and three in the morning.

"Oscar, you are going to kill yourself," my mother told me, "and you aren't going to do better anyway because you will be exhausted by the time of the exam."

"No, Mother, I have to work hard if I want to get good grades."

Not everything was studying. We would take a rest from time to time. "Stop, stop, you fuckers," Alberto would say. "It's time to shoot the shit." The movement of book pages turning, of ballpoint pens scratching on paper, the coughs, the yawns, all ceased, and the minds stretched. "Let's get a cup of coffee," Alberto would propose.

"Yes, let's go," Carlos would say, finally coming out of his concentration.

We would go down to the kitchen to make black coffee, and then return to Alberto's room, to trade school gossip or discuss our favorite topic: Rosario.

"Goddamnit, sometimes I think I am going to explode," repeated Alberto. "I once stayed sick in bed a whole week, and Rosario had to bring my meals and drinks, that sort of thing. One afternoon I couldn't contain myself and grabbed her to throw her on the bed. She looked at me, frightened, and I let go. I felt sorry for her, goddamnit. But almost, brother...almost."

And then back to studying: algebra after anatomy, and then history. Three, four in the morning. "You are going to kill yourself if you keep this up," my mother warned me.

"Don't worry." But I was beginning to despair. Even though I hadn't done badly in any exam I was not satisfied. A good grade was not enough. Fives. Only fives were of any use to me. Otherwise Iriarte could take the honor sash away from me. Perhaps he had already done so. The thought caused me anguish.

"Who knows, who knows," Carlos told me. "Last year the race was between Iriarte and me, and they finally gave it to me. Maybe they can't stand him. Or maybe if the two of you are very close they will give it to him just because he almost won it last year."

"I just don't know."

"You should prepare yourself for the worst, Oscar." interjected Alberto, "Between a commuter and a boarder, the boarder has the advantage. That's the way those priests are. You must also take into account that you were absent from class almost a month—a couple more weeks and they would have retained you. Goddamnit! You two are worrying about first places and I don't even think I can pass the year."

"Aw, come on," protested Carlos.

"Yes, Alberto," I assured him. "You may flunk two subjects at the most, but you'll pass."

"Who knows, who knows. I'm sure I flunked algebra."

"That's just one, man, don't worry," Carlos reassured him. "And by the way, didn't Rosario say anything when you almost threw her onto the bed?"

"No. She looked at me, scared, and left the room."

"Goddamnit, I'd be so horny I'd be climbing the walls."

"Are you telling me?"

Back to the books. I to get first place, Alberto to pass the year, Carlos to help us both, to talk about Rosario, to smile at her whenever he saw her, to ask her how she was doing in school.

When we were studying for the philosophy exam Rodrigo came with Carlos, more to meet the great Rosario, I thought, than to study with us. "Man, who could believe it. The maid's daughter. I might have even asked her to go steady. If I hadn't known, of course." That night he put himself in charge of fixing the black coffee. During our second break he and Rosario brought a tray of cookies with our coffee. When Rosario left the room his brother exclaimed, "You sure get things done right, don't you?"

"Oh, it's all in the charm."

Alberto finished his coffee and began to describe Rosario's nude body (seen through Venetian blinds and a half-open bathroom window). "Those tits, brother, those tits. After a while he left the room, supposedly to take a good shit.

"Good shit my ass," Rodrigo said. "I'll bet he's beating off."

In spite of all those nights of studying until three and four in the morning I didn't feel confident about my performance. Sometimes I had the impression that such great effort was dulling my mind rather than helping it, just as my mother kept telling me. Nevertheless I would return to Alberto's house in the evenings.

Iriarte looked fresh and pleased with himself every morning, while I felt on the brink of exhaustion. But we remained friends.

"Don't kill yourself, Oscar," he told me. "It isn't worth it."

"Stop getting good grades, then."

And the honor sash seemed harder and harder to obtain. "Who knows," Carlos told me. "Maybe they will give it to you after all."

Geometry would perhaps be the key exam. Alberto was failing the subject and I had my only bad grade in it. That fucking Professor Reyes! We set aside Friday for review, Saturday for theorems, and Sunday for problem-solving. The exam would be Monday morning, and after that we would have only literature left.

Saturday night was not long enough, however. "How many theorems are there, anyhow?" Carlos asked. "We have been at this for hours."

"We better take a rest," I suggested. "Our heads are getting numb."

So down we went to make coffee, and back to the room to bullshit and to talk about Rosario.

"And what about your father?" Carlos inquired. "He's a man, too. And she is some woman."

"Perhaps he is interested. But I don't think that he has touched her yet. He has his girlfriends, anyway, so he's probably too busy in that department. Besides, it would be too risky. Imagine my mother's fury if she found out. It would be enough of a hassle if I did it. And what if my father got Rosario pregnant? Too risky..."

"How do you know that your father has girlfriends? Does your mother have any idea?" I asked him.

"Oh, I've been told...friends of his. I think my mother knows but pretends not to."

"How come?"

"Well...why make a big fuss when the old man is probably just carousing. If my mother starts making his life miserable he could get serious, if for nothing else than to escape her nagging."

"I don't think my mother would put up with anything like that," I said.

"Just wait for ten years or so to go by. It happens to most men. As soon as white hairs appear on their heads they begin to look for girlfriends to prove their virility."

"Even so, I don't think my mother would allow it. Besides, my father wouldn't leave her for another."

"It's not a question of leaving her for another, it's more like having drinks with the guys on Saturday night."

"There, you see, my father doesn't drink."

"Oscar might be right." Carlos said, "With that great looking mother he has, maybe his father will never feel like fooling around."

"When the time comes we'll see. Okay, fuckers, let's get back to the theorems," Alberto cut in.

And we went on, studying, taking coffee and conversation breaks. When we finished the last theorem it was daylight.

"Damn it, it's morning," Carlos said.

"I think we'd better leave."

When I walked into the house my parents were waiting for me with angry faces.

"Good morning, Mother, Father."

"What time is this to come home?" my father roared.

"But, Father, I was studying at Alberto's house."

"Don't you people have five cents' worth of common sense? Your mother was going crazy because you hadn't shown up."

"But you knew where I was. All you had to do was make a phone call."

"And wake everybody up in that house?"

"Alberto's parents are vacationing on the coast."

"Of course," my mother said. "If they were here they wouldn't put up with such goings-on."

"No goings on, Mother. We spent the whole night studying."

"Enough of that story," my father said. "Last night was the last. This has gone too far."

"But we still have the problems left, we were going to do them tonight."

"Forget about the problems. This is no hour for a boy of fourteen to be coming in," my mother snapped.

"But Mother..."

"No. Don't start arguing with your mother. You

won't get out of here tonight."

"Father..."

"No, you won't get out of this house tonight, do you understand me?"

"...."

"Do you understand me?"

"Yes, sir."

At that moment the maid came in and announced that breakfast was served.

"Mine, too?" I asked, surprised.

"Yes.

"But I hadn't asked you to."

"Now he is going to argue with the maid!" my father exclaimed.

"No, sir, it's that I don't understand how she could know that I was coming."

"Your mother told her to serve you."

"But how did she know that I...unless...aha! Did you phone there? You did, didn't you?"

"Eat and go to sleep," my father said.

That night I didn't go to Alberto's. Even so, the geometry exam did not seem difficult. On Monday night my parents let me go back to study for literature, the last exam. After the exam Carlos and Alberto waited for me.

"What a' relief to be through with this crap!" Carlos said. "But now we'll have to wait for the results."

On Friday afternoon we would have the end-of-year ceremonies. In the meantime we were free. Once we were in El Polo we decided to play soccer. Carlos went to his square to look for people; I went to see whether the Tellez ABC and Homero were back.

The sun appeared in the November sky, chasing away the gray clouds for a few days. The Tellezes had finished their exams at San Bartolome de la Merced and were already kicking the ball out on the street. The sun shone, the blue reigned in the sky, and the dark brown of the ball dominated the ground while I waited and waited for the moment when a voice would say, "...honor sash for 4-B...." The honor sash, my goal for an entire year. A piece of green cloth with the school's coat of arms across the chest. "...to the most distinguished student in his class..." To the most distinguished, not necessarily to the student with the highest grades. Other factors such as conduct, fellowship, and sportsmanship were taken into account. Were my grades superior to Iriarte's?...my conduct?...my...?

On Friday afternoon we put on our school dress uniforms: light gray suits with black ties. After lunch my father came to take us in the station wagon. The ceremony would not take place at the Calasanz but at the Colombia Theater downtown. Once inside, we were separated from our parents and directed to the front, where we joined our respective classes. Next to me sat Hoyos and Pinto on one side and, a few minutes later, Carlos Miller on the other.

"Ala," he told me in that Bogota accent that sometimes betrayed him, "Do you know already?"

"Know what?" I was startled. Any news could be bad news.

"Alberto flunked the year."

"Are you sure?"

"He went to school this morning to find out his grades and they told him."

"After all the studying we did?"

"That's the way it goes. How unlucky can the fucker be! Just imagine, he flunked algebra and geometry but passed anatomy and literature, which were the other two he was flunking. But Father Alfonso unexpectedly flunked him in French. That did it."

"Why doesn't he talk to Father Alfonso? He might

raise his grade."

"That is what he's going to do on Monday. He couldn't see the priest this morning."

"Isn't he going to come today? I haven't seen him."

"No. He is very pissed off. With good reason. Wouldn't you be? He said that he wouldn't show his face around here."

At that moment the boarders entered. Ochoa sat next to Carlos. Iriarte and Mejia sat together by the side aisle. I gestured to Iriarte and he answered with a happy smile. My heart missed a beat. Did he already know that he had won the sash? I turned my head and tried to make conversation with Hoyos and Pinto.

"Aha! What do you have to say now that Millonarios has the championship in its pocket?"

"They bought the referees," Pinto said.

"Yes. Otherwise Medellin would have won—indisputably the superior team," Hoyos helped.

"If they are superior, why couldn't they prove it on the field? What are you going to do during vacation? Cry your eyes out?"

They couldn't answer me because Pancho came by just then. "Remember," he told us, "if you are receiving honors use the side aisle. When returning to your seats do so by the center aisle."

The brightness of the lights suddenly diminished and the ceremonies began. First some words from the rector. "...and to you, graduates, we wish..." All lights concentrated on the rector, leaving the immense theater in semidarkness. I stopped looking at him but couldn't escape his speech. "...to you..." The dark red curtain shone under the scattering of light beams that came together on the figure of the rector. "...the future..." And the reflection of the lights exposed the ostentatious heavy architecture that pretended elegance. "...the memory of your presence..." The students seated up front, the parents in the back. I doubted that they could understand the priest, with that accent of his! "...may God bless you." Applause. The curtain raises and we discover the school's chorus ready to make everyone despair with an arrangement of a composition by Bach. After that torture another: a poem recited by a kid from primary. Then the distribution of honors for primary school: long, unending. First place, the honor sash. I deserved it. It was legitimately mine. Mine. Mine. At last they are through with all the honor certificates and medals of primary. The curtain comes down. Farewell speech by a representative of the sixth form, the graduating class. Duran's brother goes up to the stage: "Distinguished Father Rector..." I look at Iriarte: the light that reflects off the curtain illuminates his face intermittently; he seems calm. I worry anew. "...and the progress of our nation. Thank you." Good speech—short. Next comes a Spanish pianist who regales us with selections from Debussy and Manuel de Falla. He ends with the "Fire Dance;" the applause is frenetic. Exits. Pancho takes the microphone: he is going to announce the "student prince," their way of honoring the most distinguished student in the whole school, generally someone from fifth of secondary. "Gonzalo Gomez," Pancho reads. A short, skinny boy goes up to the stage. We all applaud. Gomez's parents join their son and embrace him. The mother cries. A guitar trio plays and sings Creole music. End. Applause. The time has come. Honor sashes in secondary. "I-A, Carlos Ramirez...Mine, mine. "...3-B (Homero's class), Jorge Hidalgo." Applause. He has come to fourth. "4-A, Enrique Boada." Applause. "4-B..." Pause. An abyss of silence in my mind. "...Raul Iriarte." Did I hear wrong? No, Iriarte stands up. I look at him from the corner of my eye. He walks happily, climbs the steps, his red hair turns redder than ever, walks toward the center of the stage, the rector shakes his hand, puts the green cloth across his chest, he takes his place in the line-up of winners. More applause. They return to their seats. "4-B . . . Raul Iriarte." No, no...Oscar Moreira...Oscar Moreira...mine...MINE. The rest of the distinguished students are being called. The second, third, and fourth places. "2-A..." They have robbed me of it. It was legitimately mine. Fate owed me the honor sash. "4-A, Giuseppe Bellini, Miguel Duran..." I thought I had understood...understood...understood the logic of the situation. There was a purpose in taking classes with other students, in the competition, in the expectation created by the effort...that way my victory would be more exciting. But Iriarte had taken first place. It made no sense...absolutely none... "Oscar, Oscar." Carlos' voice. "We've been called." Mejia waited for us in the aisle. I, second, Mejia third, Carlos fourth. I had understood. The purpose behind the year's events was to make my triumph more exciting. Something had gone wrong. The purpose...Pancho handed me an honor certificate with a smile. We lined up, had our picture taken, went back to our seats. The purpose behind all events... "All the events that occur in the universe suggest the idea of a Creator because it is clear that they have been caused for some reason. It is as if they followed a predetermined plan, that is evident. Something similar happens when one looks at a clock: it is ridiculous to suppose that all the pieces came together by chance to work in the manner in which they do. Even if one doesn't know that clocks are for telling time, one must infer that some artisan has built it. The same happens with the world. It makes no sense to say that we are the product of chance. Beings as complex as ourselves could not exist merely due to chance. There must have been a purpose, a creative force." "But why, Father Miguel, why?" "Moreira, lad, you are not going to deny that there is order in the universe, are you? And if there is order, someone must have given it order, isn't that so?" "But, Father Miguel..." "Oscar, Oscar, what has happened to your schoolwork?" "I don't know, Father Jorge, I don't know." Purpose, order, the logic of order. "Father Miguel, Father Jorge, why? Why? There is no purpose, there is no order, the logic is mistaken. Father Miguel, look at it this way. Father Jorge, if there is no order, if there is no purpose, then who am I? Look at it this way, Father Miguel. To a dung beetle a piece of garbage will seem precious; perhaps it also has a sense of order, but wouldn't it be different from ours? In other words, there is no order but it seems to us that there is order. The universe appears to us to be ordered because we are used to the way it is and we think that is the way it should be." "Moreira, what you are saying doesn't make any sense." "As much sense as the world makes, Father." "Oscar, Oscar, what has happened to your schoolwork?" "Father Jorge, if there is no order, who am I?" "When you mature, your doubts will go away." "But what will I do in the meantime, Father?" "Moreira, if you want to understand you will have to study harder." "Father Jorge, Father Miguel. Father Miguel. Even if there is order, which I doubt, why couldn't we say that it is simply the natural state of the world? I don't see any reason to suppose that there is an Orderer." "But, Moreira, don't you realize what you are saying: that inert matter can give itself a purpose? "No, Father, what I am saying is that the world is just as it is and we call that order, in that we see a purpose, a reason, but actually..." "Moreira! The things you say!" "Oscar, Oscar...what has happened to your schoolwork?" "Father, if there is neither order nor purpose, who am I?" The purpose of all the events of the year... The chorus finished their last song. I had not even noticed that they were singing. The rector spoke again to wish us all good luck. The ceremonies ended. I met Iriarte in the aisle and congratulated him. Even though I tried, I could not manage a smile.

Homero and my parents were waiting for me outside.

"My son, let me look at you. I feel so proud," my mother said.

My father gave me a hug.

I looked at Homero: two medals hung from his chest.

"Congratulations," he said.

"You, too," I answered.

"You deserve a reward," my father offered us. "Why don't we look in the stores around here to see what you would like?"

"Certainly," my mother agreed, and she hugged us again.

6

Following the end-of-year ceremonies I found myself in the most embarrassing situation. My parents did nothing but congratulate me and tell everyone what a good student I was, while I felt like a complete failure. Thus every time a relative or friend said something such as, "He has his father's intelligence," I would blush, not out of modesty but out of shame. When Abelardo Garcia, an old friend of my father's, and his family came to spend two months just a block from our house, my mother told them right away about my second place. "Imagine...in a school like the Calasanz," Marta Garcia congratulated me and her two daughters stared at me, but Abelardo just smiled and said, "Damnit, they are going to screw up the poor kid, so young and he's already on his way to becoming a bookworm. Like Humberto at the university, there was no way to get him away from those books. No, take them away from him and kick him outside to have a good time."

"How come you make us study?" Consuelo, the oldest daughter, asked.

"That's right, how come?" Lilia said.

"Because you are women. Once you finish high school you will probably get married. So you have to take advantage of your education while you can. Oscar, on the other hand, has to make a career."

We had not seen the Garcias in over five years and it was difficult for me to recognize the girls. They had grown and changed a lot, particularly Consuelo, whose breasts were beginning to fill out. They both had very dark hair and clear eyes and were rather attractive. Homero, Dora, and I showed them around and took them to our room.

"How do you like Belencito?" I asked them. "It's pretty," Lilia said.

"But boring," Consuelo added.

"No," Lilia went on, "what happens is that there are not enough boys for Consuelo to go steady with."

"Idiot," Consuelo insulted her.

They stayed one hour and then went back to unpacking. On our way to the Tellezes, Homero and I talked about Consuelo.

"Did you see those breasts?" Homero asked. "They look like two cookie jars."

"Yes, the little girl has grown up." We arrived at the Tellezes and rang the bell.

The days went by slowly. In the mornings, and sometimes in the .afternoons, the Garcia girls would come or we would go to the house where they were vacationing. We would play croquet in the backyard or listen to records. But we spent most of our time with the Millers and the Tellezes. We had formed a neighborhood team and played against several teams from Santa Sofia, a working-class neighborhood on the other side of the fields. Our best moments came when we defeated the sons of the Santa Fe stockholders at their club's field. I was particularly happy because I scored a goal on a scissors kick.

Consuelo stretched out on Dora's bed and opened her eyes. "I fell asleep," she told me. I sat by her bare feet without responding. Her soft, white legs were uncovered all the way to her blue panties. She could have covered

herself with her skirt but instead opened her legs a bit
more. I swallowed hard and looked in another direction.

"What about Lilia and Dora? Where did they go?"
she asked me.

"I don't know, I've just come back from a game."

"And Homero?"

"He went to the Millers'."

"Who are the Millers? Those two skinny brothers
with black hair?"

"Yes.

She stretched out once again, making noises like a
person trying to wake up. I asked her why they had left her
by herself but she didn't hear me—she was still sleepy. I
desperately wanted to touch her long, beautiful legs, centimeters only from my hands. The minutes began to disappear with the advance of twilight. She sat on the bed and
covered her mouth to yawn. After a while she opened her
eyes and smiled at me. "What's new?" she asked. I started
to tell her that we had won the game and that I had scored
in a scissors kick but she did not seem very interested in
the matter, so I became quiet again. Suddenly I felt her left
foot between my legs, closing in on my genitals. I tried to
stare at her but her playful smile made me avert my eyes
to the ceiling. Her toes were coming closer...slowly. With
a mixture of desire and alarm I wondered where they
would stop. All of a sudden she pulled her legs back and
jumped to her feet.

"Aha!" she shouted at me.

Startled, I jumped too, and immediately felt
ashamed of who knows what. She threw herself against
me, tickled me, and then ran away. "Catch me if you can,"
she dared me. I ran after her and caught her against the
balcony door. I tickled her and pressed my body against hers.

"Ouch, don't pinch me, ouch," she said.

"Don't make up things. I'm just tickling you back."

Her face bloomed with color, her hair became loose, and a bit of perspiration moistened her forehead. She laughed and sued for peace. "Ouch, ouch."

The doorbell rang at that moment. My arms were around her waist, so close now that her thighs were against mine and my stiffening genitals burrowed against her belly. "Who could it be?" she asked me softly.

"Who knows?"

The granitic warmth grew within my gut. The smoothness of Consuelo's complexion and that freshness of hers which I could almost taste excited and frightened me at the same time. The doorbell rang once again. Consuelo let her head rest on my shoulder. I yearned to kiss her, but because my face was salty with the sweat of the game I felt embarrassed, hesitated, and lost my chance. I heard the maid open the door, "Don Homerito, excuse me for not letting you in sooner but I was in the bathroom."

"Let's give Homero a scare," I proposed.

"All right," she agreed without enthusiasm.

We hid behind the stairs and when Homero went by we jumped him.

"Goddamnit." He leaped back, and we laughed.

"I don't see what's so funny," he said.

Weeks after the end-of-year ceremonies I still felt distressed at having lost first place. I spent entire days in my gray corners, sitting on my bed, revising the scene at the ceremony. "...4-B, Oscar Moreira, Oscar Moreira, OS-CAR MOREIRA!" But no. Iriarte had won. Everywhere I felt the voracious coldness of Bogota, saw its leaden sky and heard the sticky accent of its inhabitants. Failure. Failure. A failure.

My desire for Consuelo and my love for soccer rescued me from melancholy. I spent hours kicking a ball with the Tellezes, who were not from Bogota, and the Millers, who were, though without being Rolos. Homero and I played with the Garcia girls almost every day. But monopoly and croquet had given way to "hide and seek," or rather to our particular version of that game. The Garcia girls would hide, separately, and Homero and I would look for them, separately as well. The big prize was Consuelo. I would go into the room where I suspected she was biding, lock the door, and prepare to stop her escape. Upon being discovered in a closet or under a bed, she would defend herself until I forced her on the bed, got on top of her and made her "surrender," which consisted of immobilizing and pinching and tickling her, until she begged for mercy. In the process there was ample opportunity to touch her at will, to look at her legs, and sometimes her breasts, and to rub my genitals against her thighs. But it was also pleasant to find Lilia inside a wardrobe or under a bed. On the one hand it was easier to catch and overpower her; on the other hand, she did not have the defensive habits of Consuelo, who would on occasion squeeze my balls until I let go of her. Hours later I would still be thinking about her hands' intimate visit, no matter how painful it had been.

My father's disposition returned to normal, and he even gave us a pleasant surprise once in a while. Two of those surprises almost made me forget my defeat at Iriarte's hands. The first one was the announcement that he had bought tickets for the game between the Olympic teams of Colombia and Brazil. The Tellezes also had tickets, so we all went together in our new station wagon.

I still remember the game vividly: El Campin bursting with people, all-sure that Brazil is going to embarrass Colombia, but all hoping for a miracle. The teams come on the field and the shouting storms through the stadium. Colombia in white, Brazil in blue shorts and yellow shirts. From the beginning Colombia controls. The public starts to believe that everything is possible. There is a long bomb from the right wing over the Brazilians' goal. A fullback and the goalie converge toward it but a white shirt comes out of nowhere to head the ball and put it in the net. El Campin explodes in cheers and in fireworks that fill the sky with thunder and smoke. In the second half, Colombia scores again and takes complete control of the field. The Colombians in the stands cannot contain themselves. I shout until I am hoarse, the Tellezes jump, even my father is shouting and jumping. The Brazilians' desperate last efforts are in vain. Colombia wins the game. Everyone around us is laughing or crying with joy, and the scene is recorded in my mind forever. On the way home we all claim that Colombia has, for all practical purposes, qualified for the games in Rome. The return match in Rio de Janeiro one week hence will just be a formality.

The other pleasant surprise took place on Christmas Eve. The present for Homero and me came in a big box. When we opened it we found the twelve beautiful volumes of the encyclopedia we had wanted for a long time. We were thanking and thanking our parents when all the Garcias came over. The adults went to the living room to chat and the girls showed us what they had received—dolls, dresses, that sort of thing. When we pointed out the encyclopedia to them they looked at each other in silence.

Consuelo was the first to speak. "Books?"

"Are you being punished?" Lilia asked.

"No. It's what we wanted," I said.

"What do you want books for?"

"It's an encyclopedia," Homero said.

"Books are nothing but books," Consuelo insisted.

"But these have stories and digest novels and all sorts of things," I answered defensively.

"You two are strange," Consuelo concluded.

We were a bit disappointed about their attitude, but as soon as they left we poured through our present. What fascinated us the most were the chapters on astronomy. We spent the following nights trying to recognize the constellations. Since the window in our room faced east, we concentrated on that region. In a short time we had located the constellations of Orion, Taurus, Sirius, and Gemini. In addition, we kept a map of Mars' trajectory. Thus a whole week went by: soccer and the Garcia girls during the day, astronomy in the evening.

The day came for the decisive game between Colombia and Brazil. The Tellezes came to listen to it on the radio with us. We were all in high spirits though a bit nervous. Brazil scored a few minutes into the game. our nervousness grew. Suddenly Brazil scored another. Nothing could be heard in our room but the announcer's voice. Another Brazilian goal. Colombia would be eliminated. The game became endless. The final result was a humiliating defeat, 7 - 1. I turned the radio off and the silence was total. The Tellezes departed a while later. Homero left for the Millers'.

I was sitting with my head in my hands, completely disheartened, when Consuelo came in.

"What's the matter with you?"

I raised my head. "They beat us badly."

"What?"

"Brazil. Seven to one."

"Oh, that game."

"It's a disgrace."

"Come on, it's only a game."

"What do you mean 'only a game'?"

"Anyone would think it's the end of the world."

"You don't know anything about these things."

"What's there to know? A bunch of half-naked men kicking leather around."

"You should show more respect."

"Don't be an asshole."

"Oh. So I'm an asshole, am I? But not so much of an asshole as to play with dolls. That's for real morons."

Her face became red. She turned around and left the room. She stopped by the stairs, waiting for me to say something. Since I remained silent she went down the stairs and out of the house.

The Garcia girls did not come the following day. New Year's Eve we went to our grandparents' home. The second of January Lilia came but stayed with Dora all the time. By then I could do nothing but think of Consuelo all the time, of her long legs and her two "cookie jars." But I also missed her laughter and even her insults. I finally phoned her but was told that she wasn't in. I went up to my room and sat on my bed. I tried to read a new astronomy chapter but could not concentrate.

The next day I asked Lilia if Consuelo was going to come and she said yes, later. The news raised my spirits considerably. But waiting for her made me very anxious. I finally stood up and began to walk through the house, especially past the balcony from where I should be able to see her arrive. But the hours passed and she did not appear. After a while Dora and Lilia left with Homero. The maid was the only other person in the house. I stopped pacing and sat by the balcony window.

Eventually I forgot why I was sitting there. I was trying to relive the game in Rio de Janeiro, this time with the score in Colombia's favor, when I saw Consuelo turn the corner and walk toward the house. My heart raced with anticipation. There at last came Consuelo.

I was about to open the balcony window to greet her from upstairs, but decided instead to hide in the closet in my room. I was sure that she would go to look for me there. I would surprise her. Startled, she would shout, but then she would laugh. Such being the situation, who knows what could happen.

I got into the closet and closed the door, though I left it open a slit so I could see. I heard the doorbell ring. Suddenly it occurred to me that I might have made a big mistake. What if the stupid maid told her that I wasn't in? As the seconds lengthened into minutes, I began to think that my fear had become reality. In the darkness of the closet time passed at a snail's pace, slow, viscous. I was on the verge of running after Consuelo when I heard someone coming up the stairs.

Unexpectedly as a cold shower, I heard Homero's voice join Consuelo's familiar laughter. They came into the room and Homero closed the door.

Consuelo walked toward the window and opened it.

"So you look at the stars from here."

"Yes, every night."

Consuelo stuck her head out and looked up.

"And doesn't your neck hurt?"

"We have a cure for that."

"What?"

He began to pull the cord to bring the Venetian blind down. "The guillotine," he said.

She got her head back in just in time.

"You idiot," she laughed, and slapped Homero on

88

the rear.

Consuelo tried to run but he grabbed her and they fell on his bed. They struggled a few seconds but Homero, on top of her, finally overwhelmed her. At that moment I was going to jump out of the closet shouting, when Homero kissed her on the mouth. I felt paralyzed. Consuelo looked at him in surprise but said nothing. Homero kissed her again. This time she put her arms around his neck and returned his kiss.

For a long while nothing could be heard but the murmur of kisses that came and went. I could see them from the waist up only. Homero began to slide toward her legs and disappeared from my sight.

"No!"

Homero said nothing.

"I said no," she insisted. She made a move to escape, climbing on the pillow and pulling her legs away. My brother followed her, as if dragged by her thighs. His hands had brought her panties, this time pink, down a few centimeters. He wouldn't let go.

"Why not?" he asked.

"What if someone sees us?"

"Who is going to see us?" With a tug he got her panties to her knees. Consuelo covered herself with her hand. She was very pale. And very frightened.

"What if...what if the maid comes around?"

"That old hag never comes up here." He was breathless. He tugged at her panties again and took them off completely. He grabbed her by the legs and pulled her to him. Once again they disappeared from my sight from the waist down. A shoe fell to the floor, then another, and a few seconds later two more. Consueio had turned her face to the wall and appeared asleep, though it was impossible for her to be so. I saw Homero's pants flying in the direction of my bed. My bed!

It was time for me to do something but I remained motionless, as in those dreams when you want to go to the bathroom or get a drink of water, and you even see yourself getting up, but you stay in bed.

After a while he stopped all movement. She lingered in the same position.

"Already?" she asked.

"Yes."

"It didn't hurt."

He sat up on the bed and looked her over attentively.

"How come you didn't bleed?"

Consuelo turned around to look at him.

"I didn't?"

"No."

"Look again."

"Hm...yes, there is a little blood. Goddamnit, the bedspread is all stained with sperm."

She sat on the pillow, this time without covering herself. I looked at her and swallowed hard, at once excited and mournful.

"Homero?"

"Yeah?"

"What happens if I get pregnant?"

"We'll have to get married."

"How would we support ourselves?"

"We have fathers, don't we?"

The doorbell rang and they looked at each other, scared. They immediately stood up and began dressing. Consuelo left the room and came back shortly with a handful of toilet paper which she used to clean the bedspread.

Dora and Lilia could be heard on the first floor.

"Walk me home," Consuelo said.

"All right," he agreed.

I stayed in the closet for at least half an hour longer, not knowing why. At last I opened the closet door and walked to my bed. I sat down. Homero came back just then. He looked very nervous. I pretended to read the astronomical maps. When I did look at him, he blushed.

"What's the matter with you," I asked.

"Nothing, why?"

"You look like you need to take a leak."

"Don't bug me."

I feigned the greatest calm. "How interesting," I commented.

"What?"

"Cassiopeia. Have you noticed?"

"No. What about it?"

"Right side up it looks like a pair of tits; on its head it looks like a pair of panties."

"Panties? How so?" he asked, blushing more than ever.

"Yes, panties. A woman's." I stared at him. "Why are you blushing?" "Nothing. Damnit!" He got up and left the room, slamming the door behind him. I smiled.

But that night...that night. I relived the afternoon scene a hundred times. Instead of the darkness of the closet I would give myself what I thought should be my proper place: on top and inside of Consuelo. If I had not hidden in the closet. If I had at least come out of it. Nothing would have happened. Or I remembered instead the many occasions when I had Consuelo in my arms...If I had only taken a chance. Of course, I was sure she would have let me. The strange part of it was that I felt neither hate nor envy toward Homero. On the contrary, I felt a bit of pride, perhaps because our brotherhood extended his success to me. Why Homero and not me? I finally admitted it: because he had more,guts. I resolved to fuck Conseulo first chance I got.

The following day, however, when the Garcia girls came the opportunity did not arise and I, for my part, did not seek it. Not only that, I was also very distant toward her. Afterwards I asked myself why, for I should have been exactly the opposite, but I could not make sense of my own behavior. After another rough night, I slept in the following morning. I was dreaming about Consuelo, already half awake, when I thought I saw, or else glimpsed, a girl's body sitting next to me on the bed. Gladly enough, I reached with my hand for her leg.

"Hey," the figure said.

"Hm?"

"Wake up, dear."

I opened my eyes and with great consternation saw my sister's most ironic smile. I took my hand away as if it had been burned.

"Who did you think I was?"

I didn't answer.

"Such a cute lover-boy," she said, blowing kisses. She touched her leg where my hand had been, and sighed. "I am never going to wash it."

I tried to regain my composure. "What are you doing here?"

"Breakfast is served." She got up to leave; without turning around she said, "Did you know that Homero and Consuelo are going steady?"

"What? How...how do you know?"

"Consuelo told Lilia and Lilia told me."

At first I didn't even want to see them: those long looks, those light touches, those secret signals to separate from the rest of us drove me mad with jealousy. But I resolved then—out of sheer generosity, of course—to show nobility of character: thus I began to spend all my time with them, so they could see that there were no hard feelings on my part. The surprising thing was that the nobler I showed myself, the more annoyed they became. Ingrates.

After a while I tired of the situation. I pondered the idea of trying with Lilia, but she kept Dora constant company and that made it impossible. By then I began to play soccer with the Tellezes every day and stopped thinking about Consuelo. That is, during the day. At night she was mine in my fantasies and—on the other side of the room—Homero's in his memories.

At the end of January we were faced with the prospect of returning to school. The Garcias went back to Belencito, leaving Homero in a state of sadness and ill temper.

The last weekend of vacation. I was waiting patiently for the wind to clear some clouds that obstructed my observations of Mars when Homero sat beside me and picked up the book.

"What an irregular orbit. It appears to be jumping," he said.

I gave him a satisfied smile.

"Did you finally figure out the number of stars in Taurus?" he asked.

"One can clearly see six, but I think there is another next to Aldebaran. We will have to go to the backyard to look from there. I wish we had a telescope."

"Perhaps next Christmas."

"Perhaps."

We thought that our annual shopping trip before school would take place on the last Saturday of vacation.

So after lunch we got ready and went down to the living room, expecting to give my parents a pleasant surprise by anticipating their announcement.

"We are ready," I said.

My father gave me an uncomprehending look. "Ready? For what?"

"What do you mean 'for what?'" I thought he was pulling my leg.

He looked at my mother. "What is this about?"

"How should I know?" she answered.

"Aren't we going shopping?" Homero asked.

"Aren't we going to buy clothes for school? Classes begin on Monday."

"Don't you have anything to wear?"

"Yes...but...new clothes?"

"What? Isn't it enough for you that I kill myself working the entire day? Ah? What do you want me to do? Rob a bank?"

"Yes...but..."

"Don't argue with your father," my mother said. "If you don't have any concern for him you could at least slow some respect."

"But...Mother," Homero tried to argue.

"Get out of my sight!" my father ordered us coldly.

We left the living room immediately and went up to our room.

"What was that?" I asked Homero.

"Who knows. Goddamnit...aren't they going to get us new clothes?"

We began to lament our situation. How could we go to school in old rags (which had been bought at Christmas)? We would be the only ones. I could already see Ruiz wearing new American blue jeans and jacket and talking about "Daddy" and the country club while I felt naked without decent clothes. And we went on. It was unfair. Why were our parents doing such a thing to us? Undoubtedly they did not care about us.

My mother showed up at that moment and told us to come down to talk to our father.

His face was pale at first, but flushed as his voice grew in volume and harshness, until he was bright red and shouting.

"What do you do for your mother and me?"

What were we to answer?

"Your mother and I sacrifice ourselves all the time. We work like mules the whole day."

We remained silent.

"And what about you? Are you grateful to us? Why do we have to kill ourselves for you?"

We said nothing.

Suddenly he grabbed Homero by the shirt. "Why?"

His yell took away my brother's color.

"Answer me!" Homero looked at me, scared. Had the man gone mad?

He gave Homero a shove. My brother stumbled but did not fall.

"This free ride has ended. From now on if you want anything you will have to get it on your own. I'll greet you with a foot the next time you come to demand anything from me. Do you understand me?"

Homero and I looked at each other.

"DO YOU UNDERSTAND ME?"

"Yes...yes...sir," I answered.

"And what about you?" he yelled at homero.

"Yes, sir."

He then shouted at us to go to our room and not to come out of there until further instructions.

What had happened simply made no sense. But we could guess that something very disagreeable was developing. A couple of hours later my mother told us that we could go out. We asked her for an explanation but she only said that we had it coming for being so inconsiderate.

The next day I found her crying in the kitchen. I asked her what was the matter.

"You work hard all your life," she said. "And for what? For what?"

"What do you mean?"

"Nothing comes out right."

"What are you talking about?"

"The distributing house."

So that was it!

"We are losing money," she added.

"Wasn't it supposed to be a good business?"

"Maybe God is punishing us for our sins."

Her attitude irritated me extremely, especially when she began to urge me to pray. Nothing could be worse than a business failure on my father's part. Only death could be compared to poverty. And if I owed all that to God, as my mother suggested, praying was the last thing I wanted to do. I gathered that my father had been giving her the bad news when Homero and I came down to announce that we were ready. I could now understand my father's behavior. But that didn't make me forgive him. On the contrary, the possibility of his failure, and with his, mine, made me resent him even more.

The vacation ended and I began the fifth year of secondary.

7

No one seemed to notice that I was not wearing new clothes. Ruiz had not returned and that made me glad. Alberto had failed the year and would study with Homero. Our class and 4-A from last year had been combined. Once again people tended to gravitate toward either one of two groups. The soccer group received new members, bad students for the most part. The "serious" group added Boada, Bellini, Duran and other top students.

At the beginning I was very excited because we had three science courses. But I was soon disappointed. "Crazybald," who taught us physics, was not exactly what one would call an exciting teacher. He had been teaching the same course for such a long time that he had every word of his lectures, every problem he had ever solved, in a notebook. Instead of explaining, he read to us slowly, mechanically. Sometimes he was distracted during his own reading and skipped several paragraphs. It was not strange for his "explanations" to end in complete incoherence. Apart from his bad presentation and organization, and his uncanny talent for selecting the most boring aspects of physics, he had the policy of lowering the grade of those who asked "annoying" questions (most of mine, for example).

It did not take long to see that Martinez, who taught us psychology and chemistry, was even worse than Crazybald. One time he assigned a project about mental illness. I researched every bit of information that could be of any use for the project, and completed a twenty-five page report, of which I felt very proud. When the deadline came I realized that my report was at least three times longer than any other. That day I even smiled at Martinez, thinking about how much he was going to appreciate my work.

The wretch gave the projects back without having read them. He simply checked the names of those who had turned them in.

"Sir," I called from the back of the room.

"What do you want ?" he asked me.

"Aren't you going to read my report?"

"I do as I see fit, young man."

"In that case, excuse me," I said, walking toward the front of the room. I came to the wastepaper basket and there, to everyone's amazement, tore my report to pieces.

"How dare you!" he shouted. "Get out!"

So I was thrown out of class for the first time ever. Since I had nowhere to go, I stayed near the door. Martinez kept on shouting but I could not make his words out. A few minutes later Carlos Miller joined me. "What a stupid son-of-a-bitch!" Carlos said.

"Yes.

At that moment Pancho came by and threw himself upon us with his little book: We were punished that Saturday.

Martinez was at his worst in chemistry. He would send a student to the board and ask him for some formula or other. The student would write it and then Martinez would say, "Throw some water on it. Throw some water on it." As if we were firemen. So we would write "+H_2O" and try to figure out what would come of it. It was not very difficult for him to teach: Write a formula. "Throw some water on it."

One day Carlos Miller went to the board and upon hearing the usual request took a little plastic bottle out of his pocket. He squeezed it and water spurted on the formula written on the board. We were startled. Martinez opened his mouth in amazement. Carlos then let himself go and emptied the bottle. The dark spot expanded over the board and began to drip. A poorly contained snicker was heard throughout the room. Martinez' face was red, as was Carlos'. Then it became white. "You miserable punk!" he shouted.

Carlos sort of laughed, but his sort-of-laugh sounded scared.

"Get out of my sight!" Martinez ordered.

Carlos complied immediately.

Martinez tried to say something but choked. The snickers became boisterous laughter. No one could help it.

Tears jumped to Martinez's eyes. Once again he tried to speak but could not. He tried to use the eraser on the spot of water and we laughed even harder. He then walked toward the door, went out, and slammed it.

We heard more shouting and then silence, a long silence. After a while Martinez came back with Carlos and with Pancho. Carlos was very pale. He raised his desk top, took all his books out and put the lock in his pocket. Without looking at anyone he left. Pancho stood in front of the board. The formula could still be seen, as could the dripping chalk. He shook his head and, without saying a word, left the room.

The silence seemed to have become permanent. Martinez observed us, one by one. He finally spoke, "What else do you have in mind?"

A few of us smiled, but no one dared to laugh.

"Let's see! Don't you have any guts?" He looked at me. "What are you going to do, Moreira?"

The bell rang and we went out to recess.

At the end of the school day Homero and I accompanied Rodrigo to his home. Carlos was calm, even allowing himself a smile. But Mrs. Miller was in a very bad mood, smoking cigarette after cigarette.

"What do you think about this, Oscar?" she asked.

I didn't know what to answer, but fortunately she continued. "How can they let an idiot like that teach at a school like El Calasanz? Ah? As if we didn't pay an enormous tuition. Anyone would think that those priests could allow themselves the luxury of hiring someone good. What do you think?"

"I think you are absolutely right."

"I don't believe the priests really know," Carlos said. "He has them fooled."

"Come on," Rodrigo said, "the only thing those priests care about is money."

"Well," Carlos remarked, "now we are tied: one expulsion each."

Everyone but his mother laughed.

"We can't let this stand. As soon as your father gets here we're going to see the rector."

After a while we said goodbye and walked home.

"Goddamnit," Homero comented. "If one of us were kicked out, our father would kill him."

I thought he was right but didn't say anything.

The next day Carlos was back in class. During recess we did nothing but laugh at Martinez.

The level of instruction at El Calasanz was generally high. But this one shortcoming affected me considerably. If it hadn't been for the chapters on astronomy in my encyclopedia, I might have ended up hating science. When I exhausted the material in the encyclopedia I obtained several books on cosmology, relativity, and other related topics. Homero did not read them but was always willing to discuss the aspects that interested me the most.

I would lie down on my green bed in my gray room to let my mind fill with stars, with galaxies, with endless possibilities. I would think about the billions of planets like, or almost like, Earth, about the beings that would inhabit them, about the civilizations more advanced than ours. At some point I asked myself this question: if those advanced beings had an opportunity to meet us, what would they think of us? What would they think of our religious customs? The answer was finally inescapable: they would think that we were a bunch of superstitious savages. As the Europeans thought of the rest of the world during the centuries of colonization. They would classify us as irrational for believing in such garbage. Garbage? My heart missed a beat. How could I say this so lightly? But I had not said it lightly. On the contrary, I had distilled it from my mind with bitterness, with uneasiness. What would happen to my life? Without God I did not belong in my family, in my school, in my country, anywhere.

I am mad, I told myself. This will pass. Why should those superior beings be atheists? They might not only believe in God but also have arguments at their disposal that would assuage doubts like mine, that would make them seem ridiculous.

I thought about Father Miguel. "Moreira, kid, Moreira," he would tell me, "you have to look at things with more faith." And about Father Jorge. I could almost see his forehead wrinkle with worry. I could almost feel the pressure of his hand on my shoulder.

Could I believe that this universe, so immense, perhaps infinite, had been created for our benefit? Impossible. For us who scarcely exist in time and space compared to the rest of the universe? For us who amount to so little on one small planet of a star that amounts to so little among many more thousands of millions of stars in our galaxy? In our galaxy that...? My God! God? Such insignificance! And they accused the atheists of arrogance! It was necessary to believe in all this to even consider the Christian God. It seemed absurd.

Once my way of thinking was changed I could not imagine a return to what I now perceived to be an act of intellectual barbarism. Savages! Savages with Bach and bells instead of jungle drums. It all seemed like a fairy tale. What was I going to do? Pretend to believe so as not to disturb anyone and so no one would disturb me? It sounded dishonest. Well, wasn't that what the skeptics did, according to the philosophy instructor? At the end of the discussion they went down the stairs and out the door like everybody else. No, this was different. From honest doubts I had passed to an honest certainty. There was no God. Could I tell Father Jorge? My mother?

All the arguments I had attacked in days past were mere details. Only one thing was important: It was absurd to believe what it was necessary to believe about the relationship between the universe and us. And without that it was absurd to believe in God. Aha! My life could not be the same from then on. And I was not yet fifteen. If there was no God, why did I study? Well, I no longer studied. But why didn't I rob, kill? Because I would be caught. And so I continued: I ate because I was hungry, drank because I was thirsty. Besides, I thought, there were two possibilities. If God was a myth, morality was another. Or else the two things were independent. Otherwise it could not be established that God was morally good, even if He existed.

Did Crazybald believe in God? It seemed difficult

to learn any science without becoming an atheist. But, I would add, there was no reason to suspect that Crazybald had learned any science. And he continued to lower my grade every month. It was ironic for me to be getting better grades in religion than in physics or chemistry. But since Crazybald and Martinez liked me so well...

I said nothing to Homero. Nor to Father Jorge. To no one. The days went by and being an atheist lost ground to other concerns. Homero received a letter from Consuelo and I naturally went back to thinking about her. If it had been me rather than Homero.... And I went back to thinking about Cartagena, and about Justina in the backyard, generating my uncle Fabio's desire, making it grow. And so with mine.

On Sunday the Tellezes came to listen to the Libertadores Cup game in Santiago—Millonarios versus the Chilean champion, Universidad. From the beginning Millos controlled the game. Two goals in the first half plus a complete dance lesson to the Chileans. The announcer, a Chilean, had nothing but praise for the Colombians, though he expected the game to turn around in the second half. Just the opposite. Millos played even better and won the game 6 - 0. Colombia's defeat at Maracana was forgotten. We jumped, yelled, almost cried. All this while the announcer said with admiration that such an extraordinary demonstration of soccer had not been seen in Chile in a long time. We thought that Millonarios already had the championship of South America in the bag.

The following day the newspapers fell all over themselves with praise: "The Blue Ballet has returned!" "Incomparable!" "It's the Millos of Old!" Millonarios had been the best team in the world in the early fifties, when Pedernera, Diestefano and Rossi played for it. But that had been a long time ago. If one were to believe the local commentators, it was about to be again.

So I began to prepare for the return match the following Sunday in Bogota. In high spirits I asked my father whether he was going to go. "Me?" he said, "I can't."

"How come?"

"I can't," he answered, annoyed.

"I'll have to go by myself then."

"Oh. You can't go either."

My heart missed a beat. "What? Why not?"

"Where are you going to get the money for it?"

"But, Father..." I tried to protest. There was a hint of a cruel smile on his face. "Excuse me," I said, and left. I ended up where I always ended up: sitting on my bed. How could he do such a thing to me? And that smile of his. As if he were getting even with me. For some time he had not given either Homero or me any money, not for movies, for clothing, for anything. He acted differently toward Dora and the baby. He asked Dora every Sunday, in front of us, whether she would like to go to a matinee movie. She always liked to, didn't she? He would then take his bill-fold out slowly, as if he wanted to ensure that we did not miss the slightest detail. He would choose a couple of bills and give them to my sister. "The change is for candy," he would add. He never offered any to us. Since I was not interested in matinees, I never asked him. Homero did, once. "That picture is not for you," he answered dryly.

I had not really paid much attention to that little Sunday ceremony of his. But now I thought that he performed it as much to taunt us as to please Dora. Why was he doing this?

I decided to ask my mother for money.

"How much?" she asked. When I told her she said that she did not have that kind of money.

"But what am I going to do? I can't miss this game for anything in the world."

"Why don't you ask your father?"

"He doesn't want to give me any."

"He must have his reasons, Oscar."

"What reasons could he have?"

"Look, your father is in a difficult situation. Don't bother him."

I was in a bad mood all week long. But Ciro came to the rescue Saturday: they had an extra courtesy pass for me. The next day we went to El Campin to see Millonarios win 1 - 0 in a rather mediocre game. Little was seen of the greatness it had demonstrated the previous Sunday in Chile.

On my way home I saw my father drive away in an old Chevrolet. I thanked the Tellezes and said goodbye. Once in the garage, I saw that the station wagon was missing. I asked my mother about it.

"Your father sold it."

"He sold it? But why?"

"So we can eat."

Disturbed, I went to sit on my bed.

Millonarios made it to the semifinals but didn't fare well. They managed a scoreless tie with Olympia, the Paraguayan champion, in Bogota, but one week later they were routed without pity in Asuncion, 5 - 1. During the weeks that followed Pinto kept telling me that my favorite bums had dishonored our country.

With Boada and Bellini in the same class it would have been very difficult to compete for first place. Not that I really wanted to try. I simply could not experience anew the hopes and the frustrations of the previous year. Even so, I was getting good grades and things were going well in general, with the one exception that I had not been included in the class team. I was too short and too skinny and did not play well enough to mix with the champions of '59.

From Pancho's point of view things were not going well at all, at least as far as our class was concerned. First it was Carlos and his little water bottle. And then a whole wave of incidents. Some were small. Hopita Casas, for example, took to reading Western paperbacks during class, and being so absentminded, often forgot himself and started mumbling the lines he was reading. From time to time, those of us sitting next to him could hear phrases like "and pierced his heart with a shot." But one day in literature class he read loudly and clearly: "Get your hands up!"

The rector practically leaped in his seat.

"Bang! Bang!"

"What do you...? You moron!" the rector shouted. And so there was one more little thing to worry Pancho.

Nothing could compare, however, with the events in Father Tomas' Latin class. One day a couple of brothers called Huerta were making life miserable for their neighbors. To be more specific, they kept putting a live frog down the others' shirts. People put up with it because Father Tomas was not very good at making distinctions when his terrible temper got the best of him. All except Perez, that is, who hit one of the brothers in the face with the frog.

"What is the matter?" Father Tomas inquired.

No one spoke. The frog had disappeared from sight. Father Tomas returned to the translation.

The other Huerta grabbed the frog, put a firecracker in its mouth, secured it with adhesive tape, lighted the fuse and prepared to throw the frog in Perez' direction.

He expected that Perez would be forced to catch the frog and put the fuse out before the firecracker went off. But Father Tomas saw him and a flustered Huerta dropped the frog. The animal took gigantic leaps in the aisle, out of terror, I imagine, straight toward the priest's desk. With each leap the priest's eyes grew bigger and bigger. About two meters from his desk it exploded. All the windows in the building shook. The ones in our room nearly broke. It was a nauseating business: smoke, blood and guts flying all over the place, Father Tomas with his eyes fixed wide open, and then students wiping themselves off.

In a few seconds Pancho came running in, "What happened? What happened?"

No one could tell him in the midst of such confusion. Father Tomas went past Pancho without answering, grabbed the doorknob, then suddenly let go of it and threw up right in the middle of the doorway. When he was through he looked at Pancho with tears in his eyes, jumped over the puddle, and fled.

I thought Pancho would go crazy. But he composed himself and ordered us to go out into the hall. There we found the other classes. Pancho blew his whistle and told them to go back to class. When he found out what had happened he threw the Huertas out of school. He then directed us to the basketball court, where he dressed us down as he never had before.

The question of money, or rather the lack of money, was becoming critical. It had caught my father's fancy not to give us the monthly tuition money on time. The Escolapians would wait five days and then begin to ask questions. Pancho would call us aside and request an explanation. What could we tell him? That we had forgotten it, that my father was on a business trip, that.... The first time, I almost wept from shame. And it was worse from then on.

Once at home, we would ask my father for the money.

"I don't have any!" he would shout.

"But what are we going to do?"

My mother would call us aside and beg us not to bother him.

The distributing house was not going well. We were living off the money from the sale of the station wagon.

But what were we going to do? And if the money was already in the bank, why couldn't he take it out on the first of the month rather than the tenth or the twelfth? Besides, why weren't there any delays with Dora's tuition money?

I sometimes found my mother crying. But as.soon as she noticed me she would dry her tears. Whenever the baby saw her this way he felt frightened and came close to console her. And if for some reason she wouldn't stop, the baby would end up crying too. Then she would hug him and cry even more. But in the presence of the older children she always managed to compose herself. To our queries she answered that it was nothing, or that she was crying over her mother's death. Since her mother had been dead many years we never believed her.

She borrowed money everywhere and bought on credit to put some food on our plates. She already owed money to all the stores in the neighborhood. She even owed money to the maid. When my father found out he became furious, but she would answer that she had no alternative—we had to eat. Little by little the quality and the quantity of food diminished. Instead of adapting I became more demanding. If there was something I didn't like, I would refuse to eat it. Especially at lunch. At dinner time I did not dare, for I would not put it past my father to force me to clean my plate. My father took great care not to hurt my mother: He hurt us.

We hurt her.

My mother sometimes begged me to eat lunch even if I did not like it.

I found it painful. I could not bear what I took to be her loss of pride and self-assurance. So I would refuse even more. She would avert her eyes so I could not see her tears. Ah, if she had looked at me! She would have seen tears come to my eyes too.

But once in a while she would threaten me with telling my father. I defied her in silence, knowing that she would never do it. Sometimes she would get mad and insult me, but even so I would refuse. One day she threw the dishes at me. I left the house swearing never to return. I went as far as Santa Sofia and walked back. When I came in she was waiting for me with the pieces of broken china. "Look, look at what you made me do."

But whenever she could she gave us a little money. On the condition that we would not tell my father. And so the months went by: ashamed for not paying the tuition on time, getting good places but never the first, arguing with my father in the evening, and eating less at lunch. Fortunately for me the Tellezes always had an extra pass for El Campin and I was able to attend most of Millonarios' games, except for a couple when I did not even have money for the bus and was too embarrassed to admit it. Not that it was worth all that much to see Millonarios play that year. After the defeat in Asuncion the team fell apart completely. It even occupied the cellar for a few weeks.

One evening during dinner, my father announced that we were all going to take communion together on

Sunday. I was alarmed. I still went to Mass because it was mandatory at school. But I had ruled out communion forever.

Besides, our family had never done such a thing. "Why now? I asked him.

"Isn't it enough that I ask you to do it?"

"But why?"

"Didn't you hear what I just said?"

"Yes, sir. But it does not seem enough."

His voice trembled. "Not only do you lack respect for your parents, it also seems you have none for God either."

"It seems to me that taking communion is a personal matter."

"Well, I'd like to make it a family matter."

"I don't see why I have to do it."

"Because I ask you to."

I shrugged my shoulders.

"Look," he said slowly, as if it hurt him to talk, "if we all go together, perhaps God will grant us the luck we need."

My mother tried to convince me. "Yes, son, what do you have to lose?"

My father tried to smile. "It's just this once."

"NO."

"What do you mean 'no'?"

Suddenly he pitched his bread across the table at my face. The bread hit me, leaving a spot of butter on my chin, and fell into my soup, splattering half the table. I closed my eyes.

My father jumped to his feet and left the room, yelling that we didn't even give him the right to eat in peace. I did not touch what was left of the soup, but ate everything else because I was very hungry.

When I had finished he sent for me. He then threatened me with all sorts of physical violence if I didn't join them at communion time.

I was still determined not to attend Mass. But as the days went by I began to think that opposing him was not worthwhile. In his present mental state he was capable of twisting my arm all the way to the church, and once there, of kicking me if I did not take communion. Of course, it would be incredible for him to do such a thing. But I did not dare give him the chance to lower himself still more. Not in front of other people. Besides, I was afraid of him.

But wasn't my acquiescence a dishonest act? To take communion when I no longer believed in those things? But why not? What did it matter? Who was going to judge me? Posterity? Who cared about it? I was not going to have a day of reckoning, of that I was sure. Was it worth the trouble I was getting into?

Sunday I took communion with my family. Upon receiving the host, I said, "Son-of-a-bitch," but so low that the priest did not hear me. Though I believe that Homero, kneeling next to me, understood my words, for he tensed visibly. Or could it be that my brother was afflicted by a crisis of "intellectual honesty" as well? I bit into the host. All in vain. I could not escape the humiliation.

8

The autumn rains started, giving the city a cold, humid, gray, endless heaviness, dirtying the ugly concrete boxes of El Polo Club. Our clothes started to look old, our shoe soles to develop holes that absorbed the filthy water of the streets.

My "intellectual honesty" already lost, I only had my chastity left. This time the trip to the bathroom didn't go to waste. Thinking of Consuelo, and sometimes Justina, I began a long chain of solitary sins. Even as a new atheist I had preserved scruples about living up to the "highest standards of conduct" (although why they would not have applied in the case of Consuelo I could not answer). And did I make up for lost time! Years of restraint had built up an immense reservoir of desire. White phlegm now cascaded down with the torrent of the toilet.

My fears also began immediately. What if someone saw me through the skylight? What if my mother suspected something? But who was going to climb up to the roof? Particularly when it rained so much? My mother suspected something anyway. Otherwise her insistence on our bedroom door being unlocked could not be explained. Sometimes she did not want us to close it at all. But we closed it, and also locked it. Not because we intended to masturbate there. But because we cherished our privacy. Besides, the bathroom was the best place for that. In our room we would be stuck with the evidence. I say "we" because I am sure that Homero had begun years earlier. We never talked about it, but sometimes took turns going to the bathroom.

What a great relief! Not only physical but mental. Now I felt more comfortable around my older classmates, the corrupt of yesteryear. For them the topic was a source of great fun. It was rumored that Bellini and others had held a contest one weekend to determine who could do it the most times in an hour. Perez was the winner. His number varied from four to seven, according to different witnesses. All in all, I kept thinking of Ochoa as a hypocrite.

Sometimes I worried, however. If I had broken the limits I had fixed for myself, first with communion and now with beating off, where would I stop? Was I on the way to becoming a degenerate? It soon appeared that I was.

One night I had a disturbing dream. I was coming back from school by myself and on arriving at the stream I saw that the two Millers had been pinned against the ground with knives at their throats by two hoods. I tried to help my friends but the two thugs threatened to kill them. They offered then to spare their lives if I would follow their orders. In the next scene I saw myself sticking it up Carlos' ass, much to their amusement. They did not let us go until we promised to repeat the events of that afternoon every Saturday. Now in my dream it was the following Saturday and I found myself in my room pacing from one side to the other, pondering whether the Millers were going to show up or not. I was wringing my hands nervously. Why should they keep such a promise? The worst of it was that I wanted them to come. I wanted it secretly but definitely.

I woke up in terror. I was becoming a degenerate, a faggot! When I met Carlos the next morning I was so flustered that I could not return his greeting. Eventually, however, I came to believe that Father Jorge was wise: Dreams are not worth that much worry.

This time around I would not be found studying until three or four in the morning during final exams. On the contrary, I barely touched the books. I spent my time playing soccer, as long as it was possible to get somebody else, for sometimes it looked as if the whole neighborhood was working hard. Since Alvaro Tellez and I were both in fifth, we compared what went on at the Calasanz with what they did at San Bartolome. One afternoon he came to borrow my physics book and found me reading the encyclopedia.

"You really study," he said.

"How so?"

"You even read an encyclopedia!"

"It has nothing to do with the classes I'm taking."

"What? Are you through preparing for the exams?"

"No. I'm not going to prepare."

"Why not?"

"What for?"

"Weren't you supposed to be a good student?"

"To get good grades you don't have to study."

Was I thinking that everything would turn out all right in the long run? That it was the fair thing to happen, that it was due me? That things could go wrong only up to a point? Some atheist with such beliefs!

After the exams we prepared for the end-of-year ceremonies. I secretly entertained the thought of winning the title of Student Prince, which was not reasonable since the quality of my schoolwork had declined. According to tradition it was our class' turn to receive the honor. Boada was the obvious choice because he had always gotten first place. But this year Boada's conduct, like that of many in our group, had deteriorated. Besides, the Escolapians had a penchant for giving it to younger, more tender students. So they might give it to me, I told myself.

But neither Boada nor I got it. No one from our class. They gave it to a shortie from Homero's class. Thus Pancho avenged all the headaches we had given him. Boada won the honor sash. I placed fifth and received the medals for literature, Latin and...religion. I could have died laughing. My mother was very happy and proud. My father did not attend the ceremony.

A couple of days later, Dora came to our room to tell us that our father wanted to see us.

"What will it be this time?" Homero asked, in a bad mood.

"How should I know?" Dora said.

He was in the living room. I had my ears ready for shouting, but he received us calmly and asked us to sit down. My mother was by his side.

"It doesn't seem fair to me that your mother and I should kill ourselves for you," he began. "After we give you our last drop of blood, who is going to thank us?"

"If you wish, we could thank you beforehand," I assured him with a straight face.

I thought he was going to hit me, but he restrained himself.

"That's the way it is," my mother said. "Children grow up and leave, and never think of showing any gratitude until it is too late. Then they realize all you have done for them. But what's the use then?"

Homero looked at me. What the hell...?

"You better not ask me for any money this vacation," my father threatened.

"Fine," I responded. "We'll ask our mother instead."

"One more insolent crack and I'll slap you so hard that it'll turn your face inside out."

"What are we supposed to do then?" Homero asked.

"That's your business," my father told him curtly.

We looked at him with hostility.

"Are you stupid? Can't you come up with any way of getting money for your expenses?"

"Like what?" I asked him.

"Well, mowing lawns or something like that."

"Like laborers?"

He got angry. "And so what? How do you think things are done in the United States? Whoever wants money works for it. And if someone doesn't work he starves to death. And of course no one starves to death."

"But we are not in the United States," Homero told him.

"Besides," I added, "even if we were to lower ourselves going from house to house, trying to find out who wants his lawn mowed..."

"To *lower* yourselves?" he interrupted me, "Who said that work is dishonorable?"

"Some work is."

"No work is."

"Isn't it? How would you like to see Dora working as a maid?"

"It isn't the same."

"At any rate, the yards in this neighborhood are so small that no one is going to be stupid enough to pay someone to mow his lawn."

"So how are you planning to help us then?" he demanded.

"What do you mean 'help you'?" I kept on.

He looked at my mother for a moment. He fixed his eyes on me: "Yes, help. I want you to get a job."

"What?" Homero shouted, "So you aren't even...aren't even going to let us finish high school?"

"Don't be an idiot," my mother said. "Your father just wants you to get a job during vacation."

Homero calmed down a bit.

"But why?" I asked.

"To help your mother and me. There is no reason why you shouldn't make a small sacrifice for us, considering all the sacrifices we have made for you."

"We don't have any obligation to work. We are decent people, not peons."

"And how come I have an obligation to work?" he shouted at me.

"The cases are different. We are still in high school."

"If you don't feel like working I hope you won't feel like eating either, because you are going to starve to death here."

"If the food gets any worse we're going to starve to death anyhow."

He lunged at me but I evaded him with a quick sidestep. Before he could recover, my mother had jumped between us, crying that she couldn't take it anymore.

My father attempted to compose himself. "Look at what you have done. It must give you pleasure to make your parents suffer. Doesn't it?"

"No, sir."

"Why did you make your mother cry, then?"

I did not answer. My mother had settled down to an occasional sniffle. "Understand me well," my father concluded. "I am not going to give you a cent. If you want money for your expenses you'll have to work for it. Not a cent."

Once in our room Homero and I gave vent to our outrage. Just imagine, the two of us working as if we were common laborers. How about salesmen in some department store? At Ley, for examples or at Sears, where our classmates could come to watch us. And after growing a bit more, we could become garbage collectors or bus drivers. Fortunately Ruiz no longer belonged to the class; imagine his finding out about such a disgrace.

And so we went on, complaining and complaining, crying over what we felt was miserable indifference on our parents' part. If they had lost their pride, that was their business. That caused us enough suffering as it was. But why should they try to make us lose ours? All we needed now was to move to the south of the city, among those whom our classmates called "Indians." Two more Indians: the Moreira Indians.

After a few days Homero decided that if my father wanted to see his sons as laborers he was going to please him. He would get a job. I thought he had gone mad. "Just to see how he reacts," he said.

"Not even for that would I do it."

Showing great generosity, my father gave him money for the bus. Homero looked everywhere but could not get a job. Why should they give it to him? Either they thought that he was a rich boy who had run away from home, or that he was pulling their leg. In a department store they told him that they had no time to entertain pretty little boys.

Homero gave up after a few weeks. But my father told him not to worry and even gave him some money to reward his efforts. To me, instead, he added the ration of hostility he had reserved for my brother.

Vacation time began to seem too long, as it never had. The Tellezes were away at their ranch and it was not easy to organize a soccer game. To fight boredom I spent my time in the bathroom thinking about Consuelo. I remembered last year's vacation and missed her. Would I ever hear her laugh again? Would I play with her again? I would not let go of her then.

One day I passed by Dora's room and thought I saw Consuelo's long legs there. My heart jumped with joy and surprise. When had she arrived? I didn't even know she was coming. I turned around and went in, ready to give her a warm greeting. It wasn't Consuelo. It was Dora lying on the bed, reading a comic book.

"What's the matter?" she asked.

"Ah...ah, nothing." I left her room.

I was very disturbed. Dora! How could I confuse them? But to tell the truth, my sister had grown a lot during the last year. Her breasts were as big and well shaped as Consuelo's. And so was the rest.

I was so amazed that I began to observe her often. As the days went by she seemed to me more attractive than Consuelo. After a while I could not take my eyes off her whenever she went by me. And from there to the games there was only a small step. Since she had to sit with the baby, my first move was to pay attention to the little one. Ruben responded marvelously; he loved the games that I engineered. And so did Dora. All three of us often ended up rolling on the floor together.

My sister became very fond of me. If my father scolded me, she no longer laughed, but worried instead. And if she saw me sitting with a sad expression on my face—my normal expression—she tried to cheer me up. Sometimes she would sit on my lap, hug me and give me little kisses.

Her caresses were at once a torment and a delight. Whenever her slender body made itself at home on my lap it brought a delicious warmth to my genitals. But sometimes I felt embarrassed and guilty. On other occasions I could hardly resist the desire to caress her legs, to draw my hands little by little up to...

Gradually, Dora dislodged Consuelo from my "filthy thoughts" in the bathroom. How I wished for Dora's hands instead, for her vagina, for her mouth, for her ass. Now when she sat on my lap I caressed her legs on the sly and moved her in circles, rubbing myself very carefully, so as not to ejaculate. Sometimes when I tickled her my hands went up to her breasts, and when I caught her, in one of our games, I grabbed her from some place that excited me, all as if it were innocent and by coincidence. Didn't she realize it? Didn't she really?

As time passed I went mad with desire for her. But I would not dare take the last step. What if she were horrified and began to shout? I imagined my parents' reaction. My mother would probably become ill. My father might kill me. But what if she also wanted it?

It was Christmas time. Atheism had not diminished my enthusiasm for that holiday in the slightest. Christmas had never had much to do with religion for me, anyway. It was a season for receiving presents, and sometimes for giving them. I considered giving Dora a present. But how could I pay for it? And even if I did get the money, wouldn't it look very strange, suspicious, to everybody?

Did my mother suspect? How? She never saw us. She would have already said something about it. No. She only wanted us to leave the bedroom door open.

I began to worry about Christmas presents. Homero and I had requested a telescope, nothing else. At times we talked about how we would install it in the window, and about the best places in the yard to construct platforms for it. But the Christmas tree was very poor that year: Homero and I each received only a change of clothes.

The following day I was running through the bar when I noticed that Dora was sitting on Homero's lap, laughing. I became troubled with jealousy, with fear, with shame.

That night I dreamed that I was hiding in the closet,
its door barely open. Me and my dreams! From my hiding
place I could see Homero and Dora on my brother's bed,
struggling a little. Suddenly he took her panties off and
they began to kiss. I wanted to open the door, shout,
prevent what was about to happen. But I felt immobilized,
as if held by powerful hands. The clothing began to disappear from their bodies as they tossed about on his bed. I
wanted to shout, to open the door, but my mouth could
make no sound, my body could make no move. And then
I began to beat myself off.

I woke up. Homero slept peacefully on the other
side of the room. Was that all I was good for? For beating
off and nothing else? Was I destined to be a spectator all
my life? Wasn't Destiny supposed to be my servant? What
sort of destiny was I going to have if I continued motionless?

Two days later I was alone in the house with Dora
and the baby. She put the little one to sleep and lay down
on her bed, face down, to read comic books. Since she had
a short skirt on, her legs were nicely exposed almost to
where her panties should begin. Without thinking about it
twice I got on top of her, pretending it was a game.

"Don't bother me," she said.

I tickled her.

"Don't." She laughed.

While getting on top of her I had raised her skirt
with my hand. Thus I rested directly between her buttocks—with cloth separating us, that is. I did not dare look
at the point of contact.

"Hey, you're heavy," she complained.

I tickled her more and she laughed more.

What if she had forgotten to put on her panties? In
that case I would only have to open my fly, with just one

move. But how could I turn her over? She would then see my expression (and not only my expression). What if she yelled? It would be best to stick it up between her buttocks, slowly, as I tickled her, so she wouldn't protest, so she wouldn't realize exactly what was happening, so at the end she would feel like an accomplice, so she wouldn't reject me. She moved to accomodate my weight and her movement made my erection grow. But what if she caught on from the beginning? She would start to cry out. But what if she liked it? In that case I could turn her over.

I raised myself a bit to look at her rear. She had panties on. White. I placed my right hand next to them, I even touched her. Two more centimeters and I would begin to take them off. My hand started to sweat, to tremble, but didn't move...didn't move. Would I remain a spectator the rest of my life? But no matter how much I urged myself I could not move my hand. I finally took it away. Coward! Furious at myself, I rammed my clothed erection against her clothed, forbidden bottom.

Dora was startled and tried to get me off. I then really tickled her. While she shook with laughter, I rubbed and rubbed against her thighs. The point came when I knew I had to stop, but I didn't. I felt the whiplash of pleasure and, a few seconds later, the thick liquid gushing down the inside of my pants. I stood up in a hurry and laughed loudly, as if it all had been very funny. I saw her turn around, still smiling. She had not realized.

I went to the bathroom to clean myself. When I took my shorts off the semen drained down my leg and fell on my socks and shoes. I washed, and then changed socks and underwear in my room. The socks and shorts were so soaked and smelled so much of semen that I decided to put them in a paper bag and throw them in the garbage. Fortunately they were old.

Perhaps she would have no panties on next time. Next time? I felt guilty. How could I have done such a thing? What I most feared when I began beating off had come to pass: I had become a degenerate. Where was my famous "intellectual honesty?" I would have to keep away from Dora in the future. At that very moment she herself came to tell me that my father wanted to see me. I felt ashamed before her. How could I have dared?

One day I saw my mother getting off the bus. The bus? My mother? A lady from a good family? It seemed incongruous to me. The buses were for poor people, or maids, or punks like us. But my mother? I had never seen her take anything but taxis. For poor people...but also for the middle class. The middle class? So we had finally sunk to that. We were definitely middle class now.

Of course. It had to happen. Living in a house like ours, in a neighborhood like ours, with holes in our underwear and socks, without money to spend, unable to pay the tuition on time. Why should it surprise me that my mother went by bus with the rest of the masses?

Lunch was served late. It was tasteless and I said that I did not feel much like eating. My mother started to cry.

"But it isn't that big of a deal, Mother."

"What do you mean it isn't that big of a deal? Do you know where I went today?"

"No, Mother."

"Well, for your information, I was downtown, at a pawn shop."

I did not have the slightest idea what she was talking about.

"I've pawned my silver tea set so I could give you something to eat. There wasn't a piece of bread in the house this morning." She went on crying and complaining. The set had been a wedding present. And after her sacrifice I would not deign to touch the lunch. Ruben started crying, too.

What could I do? I ate everything.

The Tellezes came back and I was able to play soccer every day again. I was happy to get away from Dora without it seeming that I was trying to avoid her. Up to the return of the Tellezes it had been difficult, for without money there was nothing to do, no place to go. How I yearned during those days for the forests of Caldas and the beaches of Cartagena. There was no place in Bogota where one could go. Only gray and only rain, even on the days of blue and sun. It was as if I had lenses that prevented me from seeing the city differently. With money one could go to an ice cream parlor or a movie. But without it, nothing.

We were playing soccer on the street one day when we heard shouts and insults coming from our house. The door opened and there appeared the crabby old woman we had for a maid. The door slammed shut. The old woman gave the finger to someone in the house and began to shout, "Thief, thief," as she dragged a beat-up suitcase.

Another maid who walked by asked her why she was shouting.

"That woman is a thief."

"How so?"

"My money. She owes me for three whole months and doesn't want to pay me, the bitch."

Homero jumped when he heard that. In three leaps he was next to the old woman. "You are the bitch and the thief, you nauseating, fucking maid."

The old woman wept and threatened my brother with her fist.

He kicked her suitcase, breaking open a hole that had gone unnoticed earlier. He kicked it again, turning it over.

The old woman threw herself on the suitcase, believing that Homero was going to kick it to pieces.

"Fucking old hag, if you don't get out of here we are going to call the police."

The old woman, alternately crying, drying her tears and wiping her nose with her hand, stood up and began to drag her suitcase toward the bus stop, about a block away. She turned the corner and disappeared from our sight. But we could still hear her shouts. "Thief. Stealing whore! Taking advantage of an honest woman. Thief!"

I saw Homero pick up a stone and run after her. A few seconds later he returned, still running, wearing a satisfied smile.

"Fucking old hag," he said.

The Tellezes had not said a word. The other maid had disappeared. We kept playing but I could not concentrate on the game. I was afraid that the old woman's accusation, that my mother owed her all that money, was true.

When we came in later, my mother was sitting in the living room staring at the wall. Her face looked very sad and dirty, as if she had cried and failed to dry her tears. Even though we were noisy she did not turn around.

That night at bedtime, already under the blankets, we heard our parents fighting. Homero got up and opened the door to hear better. Even so, we only managed to catch broken phrases.

"But what do you want me to do?"

"Damnit."

"...everything I can."

"...something."

All of a sudden my father shouted, "But what do you want me to do? I am not a crook!"

My mother shouted something back but we could not make it out.

The argument went on for a long while, but since we could not understand much of it we finally went to sleep.

The following day my mother told us that my father had at last figured out why his business was not succeeding. Since he could not understand why no big company or government agency would give him a contract, he swallowed his pride and requested help from a friend who had a similar business.

The friend began to ask him questions. How much money had he given the lawyer for such and such a company? How much to the financial head of that agency? My father did not know what he was talking about and told him so. He had never tried to bribe anyone. The friend could not get over his amazement. Did my father not understand how things were done? Without graft you could get nowhere in this country. That was the very first thing one learned! The friend could not believe it: My father had not even worked out a monthly "cut" with his clients' foremen. No wonder he was going broke. One needed to have the inspecting foremen look the other way when substituting a cheaper product. Sometimes it was necessary to put the cheaper product in the jars or boxes of the more expensive one. Other times it was possible to ship a fake without anyone noticing. In such cases there was no need to strike a deal with the foremen.

My father was equally amazed. "But that is outright robbery!"

"Do you want to live well or not?" his friend asked him, annoyed.

The worst came when my father found out that his own foremen had deals with those of several companies and that the robbery was taking place anyway. He immediately wanted to fire them and call the police, but his friend convinced him that it was not prudent. Making waves like that might lead someone to put a bullet in you.

My father was shocked. He told his friend that he was prepared to tell the Mines and Oil Minister himself about all the practices that corrupted the petrochemical business.

His friend laughed and told him not to be an idiot. Who did my father think had secured the authorization of petrochemical products? Who was responsible for the national factory's bankruptcy in Cartagena? The minister himself! And why? Because someone had given him a lot of money.

My father was almost beside himself. What a bunch of bastards! How could they do such damage to the country? The plants in Cartagena had cost millions of dollars—not pesos, dollars. And the people who had built them with so much effort were good people, people with integrity. It was going to be the best plant in all of Latin America, and the country needed it. How could those bastards get away with it?

His friend told him not to be an asshole. That's how things were done and it was about time he learned it. At the end of last night's argument my parents had agreed that it would be better to sell the distributing house.

My mother told us the whole story, glowing with pride. "I hope you will take after your father. There is nothing like having a clear conscience. Don't you think so?"

We all said we did.

"Besides," she added, "now you should realize that if your father has not succeeded it's not because he lacks intelligence or effort, but because he is not a crook."

Aha! So she had also had her doubts about him!

Nonetheless my reaction was similar to hers. I felt very proud of my father. And not only that: I also felt great relief. As if a great weight had been lifted from my shoulders. I finally had an explanation, an excuse, for our situation. Because my father was honest!

Apparently the other members of the family also felt relieved, for there was great joy at our home for many days.

The distributing house was sold surprisingly quickly. Unfortunately it had eaten away most of the capital my parents had accumulated during so many years. But there was enough to support us for two or three months. The silver tea set was taken out of hock, new clothes were bought for us to go to school, and my father prepared to look for employment in Bogota since he had no money to start another business. It was doubtful that he would ever want to anyway, for he was convinced that all successful businessmen were crooks.

I was again confident that everything would be as before, as it had been in Caldas and in Bocagrande. I began to wish that my father would get a job in Cartagena. What if they opened the plant again? The world seemed mine once again. I was ready for everything, even for taking first place away from Boada.

A few days after that my mother received a letter from Aunt Elena. My aunt was desolate. She had returned from a card party earlier than expected and had found my uncle Fabio in bed with Justina. My aunt had fired Justina. Uncle Fabio had asked for forgiveness, and to prove his sincerity had gone to confession, and the following Sunday had taken communion with the rest of the family. Then followed a harangue about "those immoral 'Indians' whom one should never trust no matter how decent they look."

My mother worried a lot because she had just hired a seventeen-year-old maid, Rosa. I was not particularly attracted to her, but I could not say she was bad-looking either. My concern was for Justina. Ah! That red hair, red like fire. Ah. And those wonderful breasts of hers! What else was she supposed to do? A woman like that should not go to waste. My uncle Fabio was just putting on a show. He, taking communion? Incredible. He would manage to see Justina on the sly. He was not an asshole.

The news made me very excited. And the excitement sent me to the bathroom often. Three, four, even five times a day. I am going to spend myself, I thought. But at last I went back to normal, two times a day. The best part was that I forgot about Dora.

9

When I finished the articles about science in *The Youth Encyclopedia* and the books I had borrowed, there was nothing left for me to read along those lines. Bogota is called the Athens of South America, and it is said that even its shoeshine boys read Proust, but the only library I ever heard about was so far away as to be inaccessible.

So, instead of science, I began to read science fiction novels, which Homero and I got in dark used-book stores in Chapinero. Our favorites had glossy black covers with magnificent illustrations. Our world was populated by supernovas, intergalactic travels, monsters, robots, and ray guns. In general, the plots were adventures extrapolated to the space genre, but often the little books offered something more: fantastic situations, endless possibilities, and above all the suspicion, playful as it might be, that reality could be very different from what everybody thought.

In the sixth form we were the big men on campus, the oldest, the most serious. Which made us think that we could get away with everything. Of course, Pancho never agreed. That year, as in fourth, the confrontation took place over the English instructor. The Escolapians had hired an Irishman who had just arrived in the country and did not speak Spanish. The reason for such a brilliant decision was that in order to communicate with him we would be forced to learn English.

The Irishman had red hair and freckles, was some

thirty years old, and smiled all the time. That was the first day—until we noticed how nervous he was. The commotion started soon, but the poor man was so disoriented, he didn't know whether such goings-on were normal or whether he should complain. As he gained experience and learned more Spanish, he smiled a lot less. In a few months he was positively unhappy.

One day after class Iriarte and Ochoa advised him to beware of Perez and Lopez because they were queer. From that day on Perez and Lopez accosted him. At the end of class they would come near and touch him, as if by accident. Or would put a hand on his shoulder. And would follow him everywhere. The poor man would sweat. His eyes would flash with alarm every time he saw them coming. He would attempt to avoid them. But they always managed to end by his side. And one afternoon, on our way out of the building, they finished him off. We were walking in formation when Perez and Lopez started to leave their places to touch the Irishman. He was flustered and quickened his pace. But his torturers moved to the front of the line. The rest of us laughed and applauded every time either of the two managed to make contact. The Irishman looked at each door we passed, hoping for the presence of an Escolapian, but soon despaired and ran. Perez and Lopez exchanged one look and took off after him, shouting all sorts of things.

"Aw, bad boy, wait for us."

"Mister, Mister, not so fast."

On seeing them the Irishman ran faster and did not stop until he got on the bus. Rumor had it that he did not allow anyone to sit next to him.

He did not come back the next day. Nor the one after. We had a great time during his class period: chalk fights, obscene songs, imitations of the Irishman running.

We felt very pleased with ourselves, very cool. Pancho came to announce that the Irishman had resigned. A smile of understanding spread throughout the classroom.

"Oh. You're pleased, aren't you?" Pancho said bitterly. "You won't have to study English anymore. We hired this instructor so you would have a better chance of passing your admission exams at the university. From now on, this will be a study period, supervised by me."

As the days went by my feeling of pleasure turned into remorse, as it had two years earlier in the case of the Jew.

Since it was just a matter of months, I began to worry about going to college. The topic made me very nervous, especially in view of my family's economic situation. My father had been unable to find a good job. He finally had to settle for anything. And anything turned out to be a government job. One of those positions like most bureaucratic positions, in which you work little but earn little. But it was better than starving to death. Or stealing. That is what he told my mother. And that is what she told us.

But even though his new job was better than starving to death or stealing, it was worse than what we had all expected. The ill effects were almost immediate: His temper worsened rapidly, to the point of equaling that of months earlier. And then the tensions and the fights, the rancor and the lack of support returned to our home.

Through all of it I kept hoping that my chances of going to college would not be spoiled. But which college? And what was I supposed to study? According to the career aptitude tests the Escolapians had given us, I was well suited for engineering and medicine. The first one did not interest me. And I hated the very thought of medical school. I don't know whether I was squeamish or not, but the idea of having to deal with corpses was definitely revolting. One Sunday I was eating lunch at the home of some cousins who were in medical school, listening to my uncle sing his usual song: that his sons were a couple of loafers, that they didn't study, that all the money he was passing on to the university was lost money, that the results of their schooling could not be seen. That was his favorite expression: that the results could not be seen.

After the soup one of my cousins interrupted his harangue: "Father, this time you are going to see the results of my education." He put a box on the table, opened it, and placed its contents next to the meat tray: a human kidney, half putrid and very ill-smelling. I felt the soup rise up to my nose. My uncle was left with his mouth open and my cousin went on, "I cut it out myself," he said with sarcastic pride, "it belonged to a whore that died in a drunken spree."

It goes without saying that he ruined everybody's lunch. My cousins loved to do and say things that turned people's stomachs. Although, to be fair, once in a while they came up with something interesting. One afternoon one of them cut off a man's genitals, a cock and balls, and put it inside a female classmate's lab smock pocket. Back in the classroom the professor asked the girl to explain something or other. She stood up and tucked her hands in her pockets. A spark of surprise twinkled in her eyes. She slowly exhibited her finding to all those present.

"Who is missing this?" she asked.

She obviously had the nerve for that sort of thing. I doubted very much that I had it also.

I decided to ask my father for advice. Very disdainfully, he informed me that it was none of his business. His obligations toward me would end with my high school graduation. If I wanted to go to the university I would have to pay for it myself.

His answer made me furious, but before I could say anything Homero butted into the argument. He pointed out that my father had an obligation to support us while we were under age. My father shouted that he was not going to put up with parasites and vagrants around the house. Homero was so enraged that tears came to his eyes. My father then accused us of being a couple of crying faggots. What he should do is send us to the army academy. My mother protested his description of us. While the two fought, Homero and I left the room. A while later my mother came to tell us that we should not pay attention to my father when he was in a bad mood. We were certain to go to college. But I was not sure my father hadn't meant what he had said, particularly after he reverted to his habit of not giving us the tuition money on time. So I pretended not to be interested when my classmates discussed the subject.

There were many subjects about which I had to pretend lack of interest. Parties and girlfriends, for example. Now that we were in sixth, almost everyone in the class threw parties. There was one just about every week. But it was understood that people should bring liquor or be willing to throw another party in the weeks to come. Both were impossible for me. Sometimes my friends in the class would ask me to go out with them and a group of girls. That was ideal. Except that I had no money. So I came up with excuse after excuse. I frequently wondered whether my friends thought I was a queer. Or what was almost as bad: that I never had a cent.

I tried to forget all of that with soccer. During vacation I had grown and was now taller than many of my classmates. My game had also improved a lot. So they had made me a starter on the class team. Opponent after opponent received a tremendous beating at our hands. Our domination in the interclass tournament was overwhelming. And every day I played better, which made me happy. On Sundays I went to El Campin to see Millonarios, thanks to a permanent pass that the Tellezes had gotten for me. In the stadium I did not feel quite so happy because Millonarios was not doing well.

But what interested me most was the elimination rounds for the World Soccer Cup. Colombia had to play against Peru in Bogota and Lima. Peru was the clear favorite, but we hardened fans held some hope because "Marvel" Gamboa, the Colombian star who played in Mexico, was coming back for those games.

My pass was not good for that game, so when tickets went on sale I asked my father for money. He refused, of course. The game was so important to me that I went through the humiliation of begging him for it, to no avail. My mother said she didn't have any money either.

I saw it on the Millers' television. In a very exciting game, Colombia won 1-0. Every time the crowd cheered in the stands I felt a mixture of anger and sadness at not being there. A week later in Lima the game ended in a one-goal tie. For the first time Colombia had qualified for the finals. I was so happy for days on end that my worries were temporarily forgotten.

But the Escolapians came back with another round of lectures about careers. An informal order of importance was soon established. If you were very intelligent you should enter engineering. If you were intelligent enough but not too good at math you should take up medicine. If you were rather intelligent and of some talent you were suited for architecture. If you were dumb it was advisable to go into law. If you were a complete idiot your place was in dentistry. Other careers were not even discussed. After a time, agronomy was added to the list of respectable careers, between medicine and architecture.

An informal ranking of universities was also made. If you had a lot of money you should go to school abroad. If you were just rich you had three options. If your family was from another part of the country it was all right for you to study there. But if you were going to study in Bogota you had to choose between Los Andes, the best, and La Javeriana. You should not go to La Nacional—unless you could not pass the admission exams in the other two—because all the "Indians," the populace from the south of the city, went there. There were other universities, but they were considered of such low standing that no one even mentioned them. Since La Javeriana was a Jesuit school, and I was tired of religious supervision, my favorite had to be Los Andes.

I finally realized that my choice of career was obvious: nuclear physics and astrophysics. All other careers seemed insipid and trivial compared to that combination.

Of course, my choice was largely influenced by all those science fiction novels. But not only by them. Our new physics and chemistry instructor was even more influential. Incredible as it may seem, the University of Popayan had hired Crazybald in midyear. The Escolapians replaced him with another Spaniard, Professor Fonseca, who taught at Universidad de Los Andes, and who accepted the position only to do his compatriots a favor.

Professor Fonseca turned out to be the coauthor of our chemistry textbook, which I had not opened until he arrived. He was also an extraordinary instructor, the best I had ever had. In physics we had begun to cover optics, and his lectures were more fascinating than the best science fiction I had ever read. In his classes I reexperienced that feeling of exploration, of risk, of intellectual vertigo.

If I keep this up I will end up as a Colombian village poet. "Intellectual vertigo!" But why not? Wasn't it true? It was. The manner in which he explained, for example, the constancy of the speed of light. Wasn't that incredible? Was it not like letting the mind walk on the edge of an abyss? And his experiments! Light. Prisms, colors, light. Light. Light. What had been absent from my life since we had moved to El Polo Club. Everything clean, shiny, transparent. And the truth. The Truth.

I had been born and grown up carrying God on my back. Medieval philosophy had entered my veins at birth and had tried to grow within me, to enslave me till my grave. "The cause of all causes is God." "The world cannot sustain itself in existence...therefore..." "The most perfect being that..." I had finally gotten rid of all that. What a relief! But I was left in the dark. Who am I? If there is no God, what meaning does my life have? God had ordered everything; He had given a place, a function to everything. To me. To my family. To the Escolapians. To the first places. The meaning of my life had been dictated by God. Everything happened for a reason. Since there was no God, then what? Despair? Or living from day to day sustained by the pleasure of beating off?

But now there was light. Why should I need a superstition to go on living? Why shouldn't I forge the meaning of my own life? Was not that more worthwhile than living the great lie of the others? But how could I know whether I was right? It seemed that I needed objective values. And what was more objective than the Truth? And science was going to give me the Truth. The more I knew about my universe, the more exactly I could evaluate myself. Why should I despair before even trying to obtain the preliminary answers?

But would I encounter the "function" of my life in the atoms and the stars? Would science replace God? At the end of my studies, would science say (how can science say anything?), "Here you are, Oscar, this is the meaning of your life"? No. It was not that. My life already had meaning. The meaning given to it by the exuberance I experienced before the abyss of the unknown. I remember when I was little and received my Christmas presents, I tried to delay opening them as long as possible. Thus I perpetuated the delicious anticipation, the onslaught of possibilities. What enormous pleasure in opening the packages slowly! What would there be inside? Multiplied a million times over. That is what science offered me.

That is why I had to be a nuclear physicist and astrophysicist. That's where the frontiers were. It was not enough to learn everything that was known. Such could only be my point of departure. I was going to discover all that had to be discovered. I. Was it not easier and less pretentious to limit myself to learning what others had done? And then perhaps make some modest contributions? Modest? I was not modest. How could I be? It was absurd not to try to open the biggest package. Even more absurd to leave that pleasure to somebody else. Besides, I was overcome with impatience. Science was still too primitive, or so I told myself, genius that I was. One must know much more. Can't wait. Can wait even less for others to do it. That was the function of my life. And I was going to carry it out. I. I felt that the energy of a whole universe gave me momentum. A favorite of the gods? There were no gods. Perhaps the heir of supernovas and galaxies without end? The hero of a science fiction novel? No. Rather the protagonist of the greatest adventure.

I spent the following weeks as if in a trance. I did not even pay attention to my problems at home. I found something of significance everywhere. At every moment I thought I grasped the curvature of the universe, only to grasp it differently a moment later. All this lasted until the day when the preliminary selection of a career and university took place in our class.

I had announced in the morning that I was going to study nuclear physics. My classmates either did not know what that was or thought that I was pulling their leg. What for? Is there money in it? Laughter was heard when I told the rector my wish that afternoon: They thought I was clowning.

The rector stared at me. "Are you pulling my leg?" (Which in Spanish literally goes, "Are you taking my hair?") And since the rector was bald, Lopez laughed, "What hair?"

Then the whole class laughed. The rector ordered me to see him after school.

I asked Carlos to tell Homero that I was being punished, but to invent some other excuse at home.

I went to see the rector. He received me with a stern expression. "Were you serious?"

"Yes, Father."

"Hm." He smiled a bit. "Why do you want to study that?"

"I like it, Father."

"How much do you like it?"

"More than anything else."

"Where are you planning to study it?"

Where? I had no idea.

"Can your father send you abroad?"

What a humiliating question. Though not as humiliating as the answer. "No, Father."

He stared at me. "Oscar, you like to read, don't you? I am afraid that you have read many things that haven't done you much good, while failing to find out other things that you must know."

"What do you mean, Father?"

"You can't study for that career in this country."

I felt as if the ground were crumbling under my feet. I feared that I might cry in front of the rector.

He looked at me sadly. "Chemistry is the only natural science offered in Colombia. Wouldn't you like to study chemistry instead?"

"No, Father."

"We have physics in Spain. But for the specialty you want you would have to go to the United States or France. Or Germany, though the language there would be more difficult."

I did not know what to say. The rector went on talking.

"Isn't there anything you like? Look, here is a list of all the careers offered in this country."

I read the short list and handed it back to him. "No, Father."

He studied me. "That is a problem. But you must go to the university. You are too intelligent not to."

"But what am I going to do, Father?"

"Why don't you major in engineering and later specialize in something more to your liking? It isn't too hard to get fellowships to study abroad once you have a degree."

I said goodbye and went home, crestfallen, kicking pebbles all the way.

I was dejected. What was I to do? It finally occurred to me that some university in the United States should offer scholarships. The gringos were always putting out propaganda about how much they helped the underdeveloped countries, especially in matters of education. So Saturday afternoon I went to the consulate in search of information.

I had to wait half an hour in line before I could even ask my questions. They then told me that the American government gave no scholarships, and referred me to the Center Colombo-Americano.

At the Center I was directed to the office of a very kind American gentleman. He informed me that there were no programs to send Latin American high school graduates through college in his country, but that perhaps some university might be willing to help me. He then took me to a reading room and showed me a shelf full of college catalogues.

He selected a book and gave it to me. "Here is a list of all the colleges and the majors they offer. Choose the ones you like and look on the shelf for the corresponding catalogues."

His Spanish was perfect. I could not speak that well. When I began to read the book I wished that my English were one tenth of his Spanish. If only we had not frightened the Irishman away! Few universities offered everything I wanted. And of those there were only five catalogues on the shelf. I wrote down the addresses and other information and returned to El Polo Club.

A lot of effort went into writing those letters. I realized several times that I needed help, but I wanted to keep my project a secret. I would surprise them later. If I said anything now they would think that I was losing my mind.

I mailed the letters and felt a lot better. I prepared myself to wait, anxious but hopeful. How could they not accept me? After all, how many people from this part of the world want to study nuclear physics?

In those days there was great excitement in the sports circles of the city, for it was announced that "Marvel" Gamboa was coming to Millonarios. I did not miss his debut. It was a great game in which Millonarios defeated Cucuta 4-0. And Marvel was a true marvel. His ball control, his intelligent passes, and his sudden, spectacular plays were more than enough to keep me in high spirits for weeks.

From then on, Millonarios started to rout all its opponents. I had a great time on Sunday afternoons, watching the game in Bogota, or hearing it on the radio when it took place in another city. And I also had a great time Monday mornings, teasing Pinto and the other Santa Fe fans in the class.

The weeks passed and the answers did not arrive. Well, those things take time. I should not worry. In the meantime I would study optics and chemistry, would play soccer during the week, and would go to El Campin on Sundays to watch Marvel and Millonarios.

But during our last game, another rout, I injured my right knee. I had to get out of the game because I could not even walk. The following day I could not go to school. And when I did return, I was limping in pain.

Things going that way, I was in a very bad mood when my first answer arrived: a letter from Berkeley telling me that they gave no scholarships to incoming foreign freshmen. A few days later came another. A form letter from Cal Tech. As far as I could understand, if I wanted a scholarship I had to take some special exams in April, in Pasadena, California. But first I would have to sign up, and that would cost me twenty dollars. The other schools never answered.

What was I going to do? Twenty dollars was more than 200 pesos. There was no way I could raise that much money. I finally decided to talk to my parents.

My father looked at me in amazement at first. Then he smiled ironically, almost malevolently.

"Aha. And where are you going to get the money?"

"Look, Father, you know well enough that I am asking you for it."

"Aha. So you only want me to give you more than two hundred pesos now. And then send you to California, as cheap as it must be. Of course, since I have money coming out of my ears. And all that so you can take an exam, in competition with who knows how many thousands more. And in a foreign language."

"You can count on my studying English conscientiously."

"Sure, sure. And after you fail, what? You'd return here and thank us for the little trip, wouldn't you?"

"I will pass it. Besides, it's a risk worth taking. If I get it I can become what I want to be."

"Sure, sure. And in the meantime we starve to death here, don't we? But what does it matter? We are just the dandy's parents."

My heart began to sink. "I only need a chance. I'll pay you back once I graduate."

"Sure, sure. And all that to study...what is the name of that ridiculous career?"

"Nuclear physics."

"Not even to study something decent. Why don't you join the circus instead?"

"I am serious about it."

"Look," he said curtly, "I am going to finance you neither in that career nor in any other. Neither here nor there, nor anywhere else."

Suddenly my mother spoke. "Let's stop being foolish. No son of mine is going to be left without schooling. Of course he must study here, and must study something worthwhile, not an idiotic thing like nuclear physics. But he will go to college."

My father went red. "And where do you think we are going to get the money for that?"

"The same place we get money for everything else."

"Well, I'm very sorry, but I'm not going to give him a cent."

I was close to tears. Good-bye Cal Tech, good-bye United States, good-bye nuclear physics. What was I going to do?

My mother spoke very slowly. "In that case, I am going to ask my father for the necessary money. If you are not able to provide the essentials for your sons, I am not going to just sit back and watch."

My mother's words fell on my father's face like a slap. The pain and the humiliation could be seen in his eyes. He tried to talk but he choked. For two years we had been suffering an economic crisis. During all that time my mother had never blamed him for it. And all of a sudden, thanks to me, she threatened him with asking my grandfather for money.

"I don't need charity," he said.

"Send him to the university then."

Suddenly my father got up and picked me up by the collar. I felt that my stomach had been left in the chair.

"Damn you!" he shouted. He let me fall and stomped out of the room.

My mother had closed her eyes and seemed likely to remain that way for a long time.

My father's humiliation could not please me: it was

my humiliation as well. That my mother should ask my grandfather for money—it wasn't worth it that way. It would be as if I had no right. One was what his father was...up to a certain age. And even then. But my humiliation, unlike his, was gratuitous in a sense, for it revolved around a problem whose solution did not matter to me.

If I was not going to study nuclear physics I could not care less whether I went to the university or not. My wishes had amounted to little but daydreams. The stars above seemed now farther away than ever. The black of the night sky and the brilliant designs of the constellations no longer looked so familiar, so hospitable. I could no longer count them as part of my world. My eyes raised up to the sky with sadness and pain. And the novels with black glossy covers turned into strange objects, as dreams one can no longer remember well.

Before then I would have tried to forget my sorrow by playing soccer. But now I couldn't because of my injured knee. I limped and moaned, moaned and limped. I did not want to see El Polo, nor did I want El Polo to see me. If I went out of the house I walked glued to the wall, as if I wanted to fuse with my shadow or turn into a brick. Open spaces were no man's land where I was exposed to the hateful eyes of Bogota. One of them! I was one of them at last! A middle-class asshole, subject to all the limitations of a mediocre monthly salary. But not exactly one of them. Not in physical appearance. For who else walked scratching walls? Who else sprinted like a bullet every time he crossed the street? And limping on top of that? Who else wore clothing so threadbare on the sides and so full of strange marks and indistinguishable colors? Nor mentally. For who else had the obligation, the job of convincing himself that he was a foolish dreamer? Nuclear physics! What is that? Don't you want to be a professional?

As if being a scientist were the equivalent of driving a bus.

Oh, if we still lived in Bocagrande. If my father still were production manager. PRODUCTION MANAGER. A high caliber engineer. What did these Rolos know about such things? City of soot and rain.

Every time my mother told me not to worry, that I would go to college, I felt even more humiliated. Of course. Did not all Bogotanians go to college?

And when I thought that things could not get any worse, I found out that my father had sold the Chevy. From then on he would take the bus. The production manager! In one of those ramshackle contraptions. And the driver shouting at him not to fuck around and move to the back. There was a reason, of course. He had bought a taxi with the money, affiliated it with a company, and hired a driver. With the profits he would be able to buy more taxis in a couple of years. If everything went well he might end up owning a taxi company. And then...

Since he was optimistic and generous he decided to make peace with me. And how! He gave me money to go to my class' spiritual retreat. As if I wanted to go! But why argue? Atheist and all, I went to a spiritual retreat for the first time in my life.

Father Jorge was in charge that year, his first time. At least Father Jorge is going, I thought. Perhaps I will be able to talk to him about the new turns in my life. But how could I? How could I tell him that I was an atheist, or that I was poor? How could I convey my frustration at not being able to study my career? And how could I look him straight in the eye and tell him that I wanted to study nuclear physics and astrophysics so I could better comprehend (among other things) how there was no God? No, I couldn't.

The experience was a disaster. Most of my classmates' luggage included booze, cards, and pornographic magazines. Everyone had great plans for the three days we would spend in Las Mesitas del Colegio. That was the tradition. And the place lent itself to great things. The climate was warm and pleasant, just right for the blue swimming pool, for long walks by the flower gardens and fruit orchards, for conversation under the shade trees, their branches heavy with colorful orchids that spread their perfume through the grounds, and for play in the wide interior spaces of the colonial mansion.

But Father Jorge was new in these matters. He did not know about the tradition. Nor did he possess the necessary temperament and inclination to follow it, if he had known.

As soon as we arrived he announced all kinds of rules: the swimming pool was forbidden, we could not talk (except for ten minutes during dinner), we all had to comply with the strict schedule of lectures and meditation, we could read nothing but our prayer books, and we could not smoke or play cards.

No one paid attention to him. Half an hour after our arrival a neighboring peasant came to complain that someone from our group had been seen climbing the fence and stealing the fruit from his trees. Since the peasant could not identify the thief it was never known who had done it. And the incidents did not let up. That night Father Jorge was awakened by a great uproar on the second floor. When he went to investigate a plastic bag full of water crashed at his feet: About half our class was involved in a water and shaving cream fight. And the next night there was a pillow war. To say nothing of the many times he found someone playing poker or reading pornography.

He threatened us. He took our names down for Saturdays and Saturdays to come. But nothing worked for him. He caught me the first day arguing with Hoyos and Pinto, and looked at me as if I had wounded him.

On Sunday I borrowed Boada's radio to listen to the Millonarios game. It was a small transistor radio without earphones. So I started for the garden where Father Jorge would not catch me. I put the radio in my pocket and went down the stairs. As I walked by the swimming pool I saw Father Jorge coming toward me. Such was my nervousness that I turned the radio on accidentally. Father Jorge was almost by my side already. In a panic I turned the knob all the way to shut it off. But in the wrong direction. The announcer's voice exploded in the silence of the place: "Klinger advances with the ball...passes it..." I had taken my hands out of my pockets and was now paralyzed, looking at the priest with as much amazement as he looked at me. How could it have come to this?

He put his hand out. "Give it to me."

"Goal! Goal!" the announcer shouted. Whose?

I gave him the radio and he shut it off, put it in his pocket, turned around, and left.

Iriarte and Duran saw the whole thing and made teasing gestures in my direction.

I thought I had to tell Boada. But then I worried. He would demand compensation. What would I tell him? How could I ask my father for the money? I despaired all afternoon. It made me bitter to think that for any of my classmates the matter would not have been much of a problem. They did not suffer my family and money difficulties.

Disheartened as never before, I entered the dining room for supper. When the ten minutes of conversation came up Father Jorge spoke. First he gave us the results of the day's games, "for those who want to know." Millonarios had tied. Then he informed us that from then on there would be no more restrictions, as long as our conduct was reasonable. And lastly he assured us that he had destroyed the punishment list. We were all very surprised. My classmates were very happy and began to tell jokes. After dinner they gathered to sing a little. The business of the radio kept me from participating.

I finally decided to go to Father Jorge's room. He showed me in and closed the door. We looked at each other in silence, thinking of other days that now seemed long gone.

"Father, I came to ask you the favor of returning the radio to me."

"Why?"

"It isn't mine, Father. It's Boada's."

"You should have thought about that beforehand."

"Father," I confessed, "I can't pay Boada for it." I lowered my eyes. I tried not to cry. My downfall would have been complete.

But he gave me the radio back.

"Thanks, Father." I looked at him. He seemed sad.

"Oscar..." He appeared to have so many things to tell me, to ask me. This isn't worthy of you. You are not like the rest. What has happened to you? But he averted his eyes. "Go," he said.

Thus I escaped an embarrassing situation. But another came up shortly. I was the only one in my class who could not buy a graduation ring. When I asked my father for the money he answered that he did not have any to spare on junk. Why had he sent me to the retreat? That was different. That was to attract God's grace. It was pitiful to hear him say things of that sort. He who had never been a churchgoer before. Now he took communion every Sunday and urged us to "Beg the Lord."

The taxi, a Dodge, had arrived during the retreat. Everyone at home raved about how big and pretty it was. Since for two years the government had banned the import of American cars, except those for public service (to improve the balance of payments), it was rare to see a brand new model. The following weekend I found out that the taxi was at my father's disposal every Sunday. And my father wanted to do nothing but drive it. After all, he was an engineer and machines fascinated him.

But for me it was more than a car; it was a taxi first of all. Thus I could not feel worse than when he forced me to go for a ride to the north.

With my father at the steering wheel we headed for the freeway. I sat in the middle of the back seat and tried to crouch as much as possible. What if one of my classmates saw us? Moreira's father a taxi driver! What they would say about it in class! Then they would understand why I was the only one who was not buying a ring. And who knows what else.

The rest of the family were in high spirits. They had fought to sit next to the windows at first and were now making all sorts of favorable comments about the Dodge. My father seemed like a little boy with a toy. I was the only one who felt miserable. I only wished for the ride to end soon. I was lamenting in silence when I felt the pressure of a strange knee against mine. It was the young maid, Elsa. Rodrigo Miller, who found her very attractive, teased her every time he came over and called her "sweetheart." She blushed but smiled. I did not find it at all amusing.

For several weeks now she had been smiling and making eyes at me. Sometimes she sat at the table, near me, where she could observe me well. And she was constantly asking me whether I needed anything. I soon realized that it would be very easy for me to go to bed with her. I only had to go to her room whenever we were alone in the house. But I ruled out the idea almost immediately.

Why? Today I would explain that I could not go to bed with a maid because it would constitute an act of social exploitation. The way things go in the country, one only fucks women for whom he has no respect, his social inferiors: the peasants and the maids. And that is where the whores come from. The higher classes use the lower-class women for pleasure, a pleasure that is considered dirty, low. And I—besides being a great believer in the equality of all human beings, the dignity of all people, and all those things—certainly do not want to take advantage of an unfair social system.

But the truth of the matter is that I did not go to bed with Elsa precisely because I thought her too inferior, too dirty, too nothing. And all of it because she was a maid. The more precarious our economic and social situation, the more the disgust and horror with which I viewed those even less fortunate. With the most Calvinistic mentality, I scarcely considered them human. And the more setbacks, the more events that placed me nearer them, the more I detested them.

Thus her advances met nothing but arrogance in me. How did she dare think that I would lower myself to her level? With a maid...impossible! I answered her questions curtly. I ordered her about without even looking at her, almost as if I found her very presence insulting. And I was harsh. At dinner time, for example, I complained that the silverware was dirty; I demanded that it be cleaned again, because I was not a maid's son. She would smile and I would react to her smiles with even greater contempt, until she stopped smiling and went pale. Did she cry?

Did she cry over me? Over me? Why did I never think about it? I complain of loneliness. How would I have managed in Elsa's position? What enormous loneliness, the life of a maid in Bogota. Working day and night, doing the most servile things.... But enough of social sentimentalism. It is probably an "intellectual" posture I have taken up. One more pretension. The maid's case does not move me. Nothing moves me.

Nonetheless, sometimes I ask myself whether she cried over me. As if her misery were a pleasant memory I should keep in my files. And why did I pay attention to Justina and not to her? Ah. But Justina was more than a maid. Justina was a superwoman. Ah. That red hair. And that body...beautiful!

Not that Elsa needed that much pity. If she did cry over me I do not think she did it for long. She ceased pursuing me and I felt relieved, though I kept treating her as badly as before. She looked much happier, as if my arrogance could no longer bother her. A couple of weeks later I found out why. My mother had gone shopping but returned because she had forgotten something. On entering the kitchen she heard laughter coming from the maid's room. Suspecting that something was going on she opened the door and saw Elsa and Homero nude in bed. Needless to say, there was a tremendous commotion. My mother fired Elsa immediately, though not without first calling her a tramp and a whore and shouting that she never wanted to see her again. She slapped Homero's face. And when my father came home she made sure that my brother received a good portion of his purgatory right here on earth. "Dirty pig!" my mother shouted at him. And Elsa? I saw her leave, her head bowed down, tears falling from her cheeks, not knowing where to go. But she left. The monstrous city swallowed her. She might not have been able to get another job and turned to prostitution. Or she might have gone back to the little town from where she had come.

Homero? When the pain of the beatings went away he felt very proud. Proud about everything he had done with Elsa. And not only about that. He also felt very proud for not having betrayed Rodrigo Miller, who was also involved in the matter. If my mother had returned fifteen minutes later she would have found the three of them. He was a man's man, Homero.

The school year ended and I graduated. My last end-of-year ceremony was like all the others, except for the emotional atmosphere. It all seemed so stupid to me when we went up to the stage to receive our diplomas and the rector's congratulations. Some of my classmates even had tears in their eyes. And whenever they spoke they choked. Anyone would think we were receiving the Nobel Prize. I smiled like everybody else, and promised to get together, to call on the telephone, not to forget the good times. And all those around told us how proud they were of us. But was it not true that practically any idiot could graduate?

So young, scarecely sixteen years old and already a high school graduate. People should be proud of me. But what good was the whole thing to me? What was I going to do? Get a little job somewhere? Sure, a little job good enough for a poor and mediocre but decent man. In other words, with a suit and tie. And with shorts full of holes. Drinking black coffee and saying, "Ala, but what a terrible thing." And dreaming of the day when I would have the opportunity, the pleasure, the honor of buying a house, a beautiful big house, in a decent neighborhood, first class, in a neighborhood like...in a neighborhood like...like El Polo Club!

10

To celebrate my graduation, my parents gave a party and invited the Moreira grandparents and other relatives. Everyone congratulated me, everyone said how proud he was of me, everyone made me feel very embarrassed. I was already expecting a round of questions about my future, about my career, when my father made the big announcement. It turned out that he and Grandfather Moreira, both engineers, had obtained for me a scholarship from the Engineering Society. It would be 5,000 pesos yearly during the five years of study, engineering, of course. The only requirements were that I pass the admission exam and not flunk any semesters. Everyone applauded and congratulated me again. Thus I learned that I was to major in engineering. The surprise startled me, until my mother suggested that I should thank my two benefactors.

"You are welcome, my son," my grandfather said. "It pleases me much that you want to continue the family tradition."

I was brave and smiled all I could. After all, it was better to go to college than to end up as a little employee somewhere. Even if I didn't like what I was studying.

The following morning my father informed me that I would attend La Nacional. My legs wobbled. La Nacional! He explained that if I enrolled in either La Javeriana or Los Andes most of the money would go for tuition, whereas at La Nacional I could not only cover all my expenses but would even have some left over to help at home. Help at home! As in a family of poor devils.

When I indicated my desire to apply to the other two in case I did not pass the admission exam for La Nacional, he told me that there was no reason why I should not pass, that if I studied over vacation I would have no problems. I suspected not only that he wanted to save on application money, but also that he wanted to prevent my flunking the admission exam at La Nacional on purpose so I could go to Los Andes.

I had wanted to discover the secrets of the universe, only to end up designing nuts and bolts and directing laborers. I was lying on my bed, damning my luck when my mother came into the room. She stared at me silently and sat on Homero's bed.

"You don't look very happy."

"No, Mother."

"Don't you like engineering?"

"No, Mother."

"I don't either. I wish it were a scholarship for agronomy instead. But there aren't any of those."

Agronomy? Why in hell would I want to take care of corn husks? But I said nothing. What for?

"Look at it this way, once you graduate you can go abroad to study what you like."

"Since it is no less than five years."

"Better late than never."

"Why don't I go abroad now? Why should I waste five years of my life studying something about which I couldn't care less?"

"You must have patience."

"Patience? And how do I know that I'll be able to get a scholarship in five years? Why couldn't I get one now?"

"It's easier with a degree. That is the truth. For

example, Maria's cousin..."

And she began to give me dozens of examples. But since I did not believe that it was so easy, and since I did not feel like listening to her any more, I told her that I had to go to Carlos Miller's.

As I was leaving she said, "I hope things will turn out better for you than for your father."

If she knew how much that comment hurt me!

Carlos had not heard of my "good luck" yet. He was very glad that I was going to study engineering, for that was his plan, too. Except that he would do it at La Javeriana. When I told him that I was applying only to La Nacional he kept quiet. We made plans to study together. We would begin the following week, which should give us a month and a half to prepare. We decided to invite Alvaro Tellez who, we thought, was also going to study engineering.

But Alvaro told me that he was going to dedicate himself to medicine.

"Why that?" I asked him.

"Because it's a more valuable career.

"Do you really think so?"

He stared at the ceiling for a long while. "My father has cancer."

His revelation took me by complete surprise. The three Tellezes were among my best friends and I had not noticed that something so serious was happening to them.

Alvaro had closed his eyes.

"Does he, for certain?"

"The doctors are certain."

"I'm sorry, Alvaro, I'm truly sorry."

"Thanks."

"When did you find out?"

"A month and a half ago."

"Is it terminal?" I was sorry I had asked that question.

"We don't know yet."

"Is that why you are going to study medicine?"

"Yes.

"At what university?"

"La Nacional. I don't want to study at La Javeriana because I am sick and tired of Jesuits."

With little enthusiasm I began studying with Carlos. But it was the best way of getting my father to leave me alone. Not only did he stop bothering me, but he went so far as to be cordial. We even went together to watch Millonarios win the decisive game of the tournament. He was, in many respects, as he had been years earlier. Sometimes it was easy to forget that things had changed so much, that we lived in El Polo Club, that my father had a bad position with the government and drove a taxi on Sundays, that I had five years of engineering in front of me...

Since the exams were in January, Carlos and I quickened the pace after Christmas and New Year's. But it was so difficult for me to concentrate. Sometimes I recalled the studying program at Alberto's house, two years earlier. I remembered Rosario and the black coffee, and those long nights, night after night, week after week. And I remembered my defeat at the end of the year. And the fear that I had of giving myself wholly to anything just to come out a loser. Sometimes I told myself that if I had won first place things would have been different. Different because I would have fought harder, with more confidence in myself. Because I would have been brilliant. So brilliant that perhaps my father would have taken the risk of sending me to California to take the Cal Tech exam. Different because now I wouldn't have to study subjects that I already knew so well. And then I could spend my time playing soccer instead.

With the books open in front of my eyes, I spent my time imagining how it would have been if the petrochemical factory had not gone bankrupt, if we had moved to the United States, if things would not have gone so badly for my father, if I had gotten the first place in fourth of secondary, if my father had taken a chance with me, if someone had offered me a scholarship.

And from that I went on to other considerations: if I had dared with Consuelo, if I had not been afraid of trying something with Dora, if, if, if.... Anything was better than facing my boring future. What I wanted was to discover the secrets of the universe, the nature of Reality. How could I possibly find them in the Engineering School of the Universidad Nacional? And it was going to be five years, five years of engineering. At least.

That future was a few weeks away, but I could not conceive of it. My imagination came up to the admission exam and stopped there. Because deep inside I could not believe that it would happen.

I was the pride of my parents, my school, my country. How could the situation not change all of a sudden? Something favorable had to happen. And soon. Perhaps at the last moment someone would miraculously offer me a scholarship to study nuclear physics in the United States or in Europe. Wherever. And I imagined scenarios in which it would happen. I would save a millionaire gringo's life. Or a foreign university president's. Or rather a beautiful gringa who.... From there I progressed to more and more detailed scenes of such daydreams. And to variations of the same.

A week before the exam I heard that there were over 1,500 applicants for the Engineering School, and that the university would accept only 150. I was a bit frightened at that. What if I did not pass? After all, there were 1,500 others.

I went to the university to find out. Yes, it was true—1,580. And they would accept only the top 150.

If I flunked my father would kill me.

I was walking toward the bus stop when a boy walked up to me and asked where the physics department was.

Physics department? There was no physics department at La Nacional. Nor at any other Colombian university. Yes, there was one, the boy insisted. He had read in the newspaper that they had just opened it and that it would begin operations the same year.

My heart began to beat faster. Yes. Did you see? What was just, what I deserved had happened. A physics department had opened precisely when I needed it.

I immediately wished that the boy would disappear from my side. I wanted to laugh, to cry, to shout, to jump. To run. To run to find out all I could.

The physics department secretary's office was located in the Engineering Building itself. It was a rather small office, staffed by two secretaries, who informed us that the major had been established thanks to the efforts of Dr. Kruger, the department chairman. The first year they would accept about fifty students. They were closed to applications, but they would accept anyone who passed the engineering exam.

I wrote my name on the register, and one of the secretaries gave me a copy of the curriculum. There was a lot of mathematics, too much geometry, not enough of esoteric subjects like nuclear physics, and no astrophysics at all. But it was physics and not engineering. What a great difference!

I did little but dream on the bus. At last! On time! What was just, what was deserved. I was going to be a physicist. Not a nuclear physicist...but perhaps I could specialize later. At least I would know something related to my preferences. The surprise my parents were going to have when I told them. My parents! My joy vanished. My father would probably insult me. Who knows what my mother would say. But what if my father did more than insult me? What if he prevented me from getting into physics? He would not cherish losing the scholarship. For that was the price, I had just realized. It meant that my father would have to pay for my schooling. And he had sworn that he would never do such a thing.

Even if he did nothing more than shout at me and fight with me, it might be enough to keep me from studying in peace. And now I really had to study. I cursed myself for not preparing conscientiously. Now I had to do the whole thing in one week. No, I could not tell my father. Nor my mother. No one. Until I passed and was enrolled in the physics department. After that I would decide what to do.

I studied frantically, as I had not done since fourth of secondary. Carlos Miller asked what had come over me. Why was I hitting the books like that all of a sudden? I told him to shut up and study.

Even my parents noticed my efforts and were very pleased. Since I was studying every hour of the day I saw my father very little. But when we did meet, at dinner time, he smiled a lot at me and made jokes about the house geniuses—without venom—to encourage me.

Oh, if he knew. Why could not the world crystalize at that moment and remain so forever? It had been so before. And not by accident. It had always been so. Until we moved to El Polo Club.

When we were little he used to play soccer with us. We went on rides, to take pictures, to eat snacks, to explore roads that we had not yet driven—Homero by a rear window, I by the other, Dora up front between my parents, until the baby was born and she moved to the middle of the rear seat. Thus we traveled throughout Santander, Boyaca, Caldas, Antioquia...and Cartagena.

My father looked at me with pride. As before. As long before. Oh, if he knew that I was going to enroll in physics.... Why could not things be as they had been in Cartagena? Had he not promised to pay for whatever career I chose? He had offered to send me abroad. Now I could not even tell him that I had a preference. And he continued with his smiles of support and satisfaction. Fortunately my studies permitted me to escape his presence.

I had two days of examinations: mathematics and physics the first, chemistry and English the second. Looking for the examination room I met Boada, which surprised me, for I had always thought he was rich and expected him to end up in Los Andes. He greeted me and rushed of to find his room.

The exams lasted only two hours each, but by the end of the second day I was so exhausted that I went straight to bed. Until that moment I had not felt nervous, at first because I couldn't care less about engineering, and then because I had time for nothing but studying. But with the exams out of the way I had nothing else to do. My nervousness soon turned into an anxiety that increased from moment to moment. There were 1,579 applicants besides me. I should have studied harder over vacation, but how was I to know?

Alvaro had just finished his exams and was also nervous, although there were only 800 in his case, of which they would accept two hundred. Carlos did not seem as nervous. "If I don't pass I don't pass. What the hell. I'll take them again next year." Neither Alvaro nor I responded. I did not think I would have another chance. And Alvaro probably felt as great a need to pass now. Medical school was so long, seven years. What did he want to do? There was no way he could save his father. Unless they could keep him alive for years and years, until a cure was found. Was Alvaro counting on a miracle? Or did he just want his father to be proud of him? In any case, neither of us could afford the luxury.ofa second try. We had to pass.

And if I passed I would enroll in physics. Then what? What would my father do to me? To make matters worse, he was kinder to me each day, as much as he had been years earlier, and then some. I shouldn't worry, he said to me, he was sure I had passed. I already had the scholarship practically in my pocket. On Sunday he invited me to the game. Millonarios played against Red Star from Yugoslavia, the team of the famous Sekularac, the "White Pele." Millonarios won 2-1 in a good game, but I could not enjoy it much. Perhaps my father would go on smiling at me the same way he did at the stadium. Perhaps. Perhaps things were returning to normal. Perhaps.

But I well knew that it was all wishful thinking. Not only was he going to be furious at me for rejecting the scholarship in order to study physics instead—that is, if I passed—but he was also going to think that I had been fooling him all this time. And once he felt betrayed by me, there would be no way for him ever to trust me again. Our relationship would return to what it had been for the past two years. Or worse. But perhaps not. Perhaps not. How I wanted everything to come out all right. If I had not been an atheist I think I would have prayed with great fervor.

Doubly nervous, I got up on Monday and joined Alvaro to find out the results. We went to the School of Medicine first. The list of those who had been admitted was on the secretary's door. Alvaro's face like a ghost's, we searched and searched until we found his name. The blood returned to his face all at once. He became so red that he looked embarrassed. But his smile left no doubt. "What a relief," he said.

Although the School of Engineering was only three blocks away, centuries went by before we arrived there. Before looking at the list we had to go to the bathroom. And after that we had to make our way through dozens of persons looking at the list, some that moved forward nervously, others that left long-faced, desolate. At last we could read it. Oscar Moreira, Oscar Moreira...there was my name. "Seventy-five points," Alvaro read aloud. "Not bad." I looked for Boada's name. He had received 82 points. They had accepted all those with a score above 45 points, 152 in all. I went up to the physics department office to sign up.

Alvaro was so happy that he invited me to eat at the university cafeteria and to a movie that afternoon. I accepted. The longer I could delay facing my father with the news, the better.

But I finally ran out of excuses. The movie ended, the bus came, we returned to El Polo, I stood in front of the house: I had to go in. My parents were waiting for me in the living room, both sitting on the couch. I sat on a stool, thinking that I may need to move quickly.

"Well?" my father asked.

I was almost paralyzed with fear.

"I passed."

They smiled, relieved.

"Of course," my father said. "That is the only thing that could be expected from a Moreira."

I bit my lower lip.

"Congratulations, my son," my mother said with an expression of great happiness and pride.

My lip began to bleed. My father looked at me, puzzled.

"You did pass, didn't you?"

"Yes, sir."

"Why the scared face?"

I let go of it at once: "I signed up for physics."

They looked at me without understanding. "What are you talking about?" my father asked.

"They have just created a physics department in the School of Engineering. So I signed up after passing the exam."

All color had drained from my father's face. My mother did not understand yet. "And what about the scholarship?" she inquired.

"The scholarship will go to waste."

"Why?" My father's voice trembled. "Why are you doing this to us?"

"I am not doing it to hurt the two of you."

"Oh? You're not? All we have done for you, and you come up with something like this. Why?"

"It's what I want to study. What I want to do with my life."

"Oh? Do you? And what are you going to do with your life? What does a physicist do? Starve to death?"

"It's a career of the future."

"Of what future? Not of the future in this country."

"Then I'll go somewhere else once I graduate."

"Sure, sure. We can kill ourselves to please you. And then you take off for wherever you feel like without so much as a good-bye."

My mother was as pale as my father by now. "Son, be reasonable. There is nothing you can do with a career like that. If we lived in the United States, maybe. But here? How can you throw your scholarship away for something like that?"

"You could pay attention to your mother, since you don't give a damn about me." My father's voice broke.

I felt very tired. "It's not that I don't care about you. I am doing it because it's my dream. Why can't I try to be happy?"

"A dream! That's all he wants to do: stay up in the clouds like a moron," my father said.

"You have to be practical in life. You can't do just what you feel like," my mother added.

"Why don't you understand me, Mother? Shouldn't one try to be happy?"

"And why do you have to be happy at our expense?" my father cut in aloud. He composed himself and continued: "Besides, how are you going to be happy without money, without a roof and four walls to shelter you? What woman worth the trouble is going to marry a poor devil? And that's what will happen to you if you don't set your feet on the ground."

"It doesn't matter. I have to be a nuclear physicist. I could never live with myself if I didn't try."

Was it me who said that? Me? Me, who walked like a shadow against the wall, who hid his head in his father's taxi, who felt humiliated by the economic and social downfall of his family? Me, willing to foresake the security I desperately craved? And all that to gain knowledge? To find out what the universe was like? Was I prepared to suffer whatever came my way? And why? Was it to follow a "high and noble" motive? Or was it rather because I had been charmed by the vague promises I glimpsed in the little, black-covered science fiction novels?

My father could not continue the discussion. He

got up, went to his room, slammed his door shut. He did not come out for the rest of the afternoon, nor that evening, not even to eat. The following day my mother tried to convince me that I should at least think about the matter carefully. All in vain, for I had already made up my mind, as I told her.

During the days that followed my father did not speak to me once. If I came into the same room he looked the other way. And if I spoke to him he ignored me completely. My mother looked at me in sadness and sometimes I saw her sitting around, on the verge of tears.

When the time for registration came I had to tell my mother that I needed 150 pesos, and that my father would have to sign at the physics department. The news did not please her but she assured me that she would speak to my father.

That night we heard a great fight in my parents' room. We could not understand what they said but we could hear my father's shouting and my mother's heated arguing. I thought she mentioned my maternal grandfather, but I am not sure. The truth of the matter is that she went out of the room slamming the door, and went down to the living room where we heard her sobbing. A while later the door opened and we heard my father's slippers going down the stairs. There was more fighting, but after a time they both returned to their bedroom.

The next morning she had bloodshot eyes, messy hair, and the most exhausted expression I had ever seen on her face. She gave me a check for the required amount, but told me that my father could not go to sign that day—he last day of registration—because he had a very important meeting. I would have to ask for an extension. That was Friday. At the university they gave a deadline of Wednesday. But my father had time neither Monday, Tuesday, nor

Wednesday. So I had to ask for another extension. This time they gave me until Friday, but made it clear that it could not go beyond that date. Since my father turned out to be "too busy" on Thursday I had to beg my mother to make him go. So on Thursday night there was another great fight between them, full of shouting and tears. But my father went to the university on Friday and I was finally registered.

11

Another beginning in Bogota, cold and gray city. The drizzle grew within me as a mold, as if there were no roofs and walls to protect me. And so dark, so dark gray, so melancholy the world looked from the classrooms of La Nacional. Then the weak lights would be turned on and the dirty pale gray of the daylight would be replaced with an even dirtier brownish yellow.

Was that the same city where El Calasanz was? El Calasanz of three years earlier? Where for a few months I believed I was Fate's favorite son? Where the sun shone for me? Where the colors were bright and joyful? Had that Calasanz been an oasis in the decaying space of he capital? A temporal oasis in a sequence of dark and humid centuries?

There I was, among the "Indians" and their cheap, badly cut, dark suits, their "unrefined" faces, their vulgar gestures, their lack of "class" (as if I had any). There they were, with the taste of beer on their lips, with the explosions of *tejo* fuses in their ears, with the lint of *ruanas* still on their coats. And there I was among them.

Not all of us belonged to the working class, though the majority did. But none of them thought of themselves as such: They said they were middle class. I often had to suppress a scowl of displeasure. Why was I there?

But I had a very good reason. So I soon forgot, at least partly, my social prejudices. Weren't we all in the department because we loved science, physics in particular? I soon began to tell myself that the poor were as good, polite, and intelligent, as the rest of society. The only difference was the lack of money. I could not convince myself entirely, but it made my life in La Nacional easier at the beginning.

The class schedule was very heavy, and the hardest part of it came the days I had Spanish class, at seven in the morning. I got up at five, got ready, had breakfast, and crossed the soccer fields to catch a perennially late bus in Santa Sofia. The way was covered with a fog so thick and so cold that it went through me like the fear of the grave.

But none of that mattered. I felt happy traveling, half asleep, in a ramshackle bus, without concerning myself with the misery of Santa Sofia, the coarse, sullen, taciturn faces of my classmates, or the exhaustion at the end of the long day. What did it matter that the environment was so cold, so dark, and so sad if I was about to embark on an adventure that would give me warmth, light, and joy?

After the first week, the Spanish professor began to miss class; toward the middle of the semester we did not see him anymore. Little by little the class members stopped coming, until I was by myself, enduring the cold and torpor of the early morning. A change of professors was announced a week before the final exam. The engineering student who taught us draftsmanship and perspective geometry flunked us all in the first midterm. One day he disappeared (he had allegedly stolen some money) and the department replaced him with another engineering student.

We had three professors for mathematical analysis in less than a month. The course did not actually begin until the third one came along. Unfortunately. The guy, "Professor" Diaz, was a parasite, a freeloader who knew little about mathematics and even less about teaching. He reminded me of Martinez in El Calasanz. Since he was the Secretary of the Conservative Party his job was secure. He often went away on political trips and we were left with no professor at all. To make matters worse, the book could not be found anywhere. It took two months to arrive. (Like the majority of the other books, it was in English and had to be ordered from the United States.)

The geometry professor was a disagreeable worm, in physical appearance and in attitude. He had a pale face with yellow freckles and razor-cut hair. His neck was constantly moving like a turtle's. He openly relished torturing students, even though he himself was a fifth-year student in mathematics. He gave us some quizzes that no one could finish in the allotted fifteen minutes. The following day, after informing us that we had flunked, he took twenty minutes copying the answers from a notebook.

On the other side of the coin there was the chemistry class. It was taught by the chairman of the chemistry department at Los Andes. He was a short, chubby, affable man. What a professor! Not only did he explain chemistry very well, but his anecdotes and stories about scientific investigations were simply engrossing. And he liked to speculate about what the future held. I was fascinated. When I read the book later it seemed very easy.

We learned that he was teaching us for free because he did not want to miss having something to do with the first generation of Colombian physicists. He would have liked to receive some money for his time, eight hours of class a week, of course, but his contract with Los Andes prevented him from earning money at another university.

I was so absorbed in his class that it took several weeks for me to notice that the majority of the students did not have the slightest interest in it and paid very little attention. That surprised me at first, but in the end it opened my eyes to the nature of my classmates and the rest of the department.

I had assumed that all the physics students were scientists by love, that we all had similar dreams, concerns, and aspirations. But it was not so. Of the 50 that started the year, 37 had applied to engineering, not to physics. Of the 37, I was the only one who had changed out of love for science. The rest had done it because they had flunked the admission exams and the physics department had offered to take them in. Few of them showed any inclination toward those scientific topics that caused such passion in me. Whenever I started to discuss anything like the exploration of the planets or the origin of the universe they thought I was nuts. They nicknamed me "The Martian." Of the 13 that had applied to physics, only six passed. The others had been accepted anyway. And several of the thirteen had flunked out of engineering the year before. They had gotten into physics because they believed it would resemble engineering and perhaps later on they would be able to return to their true career. Such hope was prevalent among my classmates.

The 50 students were divided into two sections. There were very few true "scientists" in mine. Three of them formed a distinct group: a tall one with kinky hair and big glasses, Ordonez, whose enormous Goofy-like feet tripped anyone who walked next to him; Lopez, average physically and mentally, who laughed as if he had the hiccups; and a short, blonde one, several years older than the other two, who was called "The Swiss." Since the three walked toward Caracas Avenue, where I took my bus home, and since they were practically the only ones who cared to discuss interesting subjects, I sometimes joined them.

There was also a guy named Alba, from Girardot, who seemed to be a nice person, but who spoke too loudly and who created a disturbance every time he laughed. His worst problem, though, was that he associated with the most vulgar and boorish man to come from the Coast, Black Sanchez. Since it rained often we spent our breaks under a portico, so there was no way to keep from hearing Sanchez's stories. He used to tell us, for example, about his visits to an aunt of his in Barranquilla. His aunt was very fond of him, treated him to lunch, and so on. Whenever she went shopping she would ask him to take care of the house, to which he would agree with pleasure. The aunt had three daughters and he had laid them all, including the youngest, who was only seven years old. The oldest was fourteen. And his cousins didn't say anything? No. The oldest one already liked it. The other two thought it was a secret game. The bastard would laugh then. When asked whether his conscience ever bothered him he would answer that that's what cousins were for.

He also had another aunt who liked to have it up her rear. Sometimes she would call him over and offer him twenty pesos for "helping." And he "helped" her. The majority loathed listening to him. But he went on with his routine every day. And every time he finished telling one, Alba's raucous laughter made the building shake. When Black Sanchez was not present, Alba also said that he was repulsed by it all. But he continued cheering Black on. Some said that Black was making it all up. He just took pleasure in shocking us. But no one was very sure about that.

One day he told us that when he was in fifth of secondary his gang sometimes went to the country rather than to school. They went to a particular ranch that had a lot of calves, jumped over the fence, took the calves by the rear and fucked them. "Veal a la Coast," he said. A few weeks later the calves already knew what they were coming for and put out. They liked it, they liked it, he swore. When someone remarked that it was disgusting, he answered that "a hole is a hole." And proceeded to tell us what people did with animals: donkeys, dogs, and even chickens. And not only men, there were women who liked donkeys and big dogs. Somebody asked him whether he had ever had relations with men, and he said he had. Ass that came forth, ass that he fucked.

One rainy morning a guy named Garcia could not stand it any longer and yelled at Black Sanchez to shut up and called him a son of a bitch. Black Sanchez, tall and strong, threw himself upon him, punched him hard, and threw him in the mud. When Garcia tried to get up he met with a kick on the chest that turned him over and flattened him again. There, crying in his blood and fear, he stayed under the rain, a pitiful spectacle for the cowardly eyes of his classmates. Nobody moved because we all dreaded Black. We had seen him sadistically beat up students from other departments. His smile grew as did the fear on his opponent's face.

Since Black met with hostile silence after humiliating Garcia, he shouted at us, "He had no right to call me a son of a bitch. No one insults my mother." A few minutes later he left for class and several people helped poor Garcia

Garcia was another true "physicist," though not one of those who had passed the exam. There was such a preponderance of failed engineers in our department that the bad fame extended not only throughout La Nacional, but also to La Javeriana and Los Andes. Once in a while I met classmates from El Calasanz, and as soon as I told them that I was in physics they said, "Aha, so you flunked the engineering exam. And you used to be such a good student."

Besides the trio (Lopez, Ordonez, and The Swiss), Alba, and Garcia, there was another scientist in our section. Her name was Antonia Nieto and she was called La Tona. She was rather tall, dark, and had enormous tits and ass. Many found her very sensual. I thought she looked like a vulgar maid. La Tona said that science fascinated her, but as soon as I started talking about anything of interest her eyes would go blank with boredom. She was the one who nicknamed me Martian. The guys from the South spent their time trying to look up her skirt whenever she went up the stairs. When she was on the first floor they went up to the second and strained their eyes to enjoy whatever her décolletage permitted from that angle. No one looked at her face, for apart from being ugly it sported crooked teeth and a dark mustache.

Her physical qualities aside, she was not suited for science because she lacked imagination and suffered from chronic stupidity and laziness. I know it well, for she was my partner in chemistry lab. I had to do everything while she talked to the assistant. I preferred it that way because when she did try to help things would go wrong and even end up in disaster. One day, when we were working with a boric compound, she did not put the rubber plug on the test tube, as the instructions clearly called for. When the heat was applied to it, the test tube ignited in big flames and the entire apparatus exploded. I put the fire out, barely, as she howled all over the place. The compound is used in tear gas, so in a few minutes 50 of us and 150 engineers were weeping our way out of the building. All year long I was afraid of having.my face blown off because of her.

There were two more women in the other section.

One of them was "Southern," as was La Tona. The other one was "decent."

Although Alba was friendly toward me, and the trio allowed me to participate in their conversations, I did not feel comfortable in the department. On the one hand, because of my age—I was sixteen whereas the rest ranged from nineteen to thirty. On the other hand, the trio provided some intellectual stimulation, though not much. The professors, with the exception of the chemistry one, provided nothing. And the wealth he had to give could not possibly interest all those frustrated engineers.

That was during the day. At night came the confrontations with my father. He could not forgive me for not enrolling in engineering. And what saddened me most was that my career resembled more each day the one I detested. I had expected paradise and had found only boredom and lack of imagination. After hearing my father yell that I should put my feet on the ground, that only idiots walked on clouds, that in this country scientists were fit only for death by starvation, how could I prepare for the class of the maggot that taught us geometry or for that of the reptile who allegedly lectured on mathematical analysis? And to make matters worse, when the books finally came my father refused to give me money to buy them. "If you need them so much get a job!" he shouted.

My enthusiasm began to wane. Just in time for the midterm examinations. In spite of the disappointments experienced I still believed that the department was something special, that because we were the first generation of physicists in the country the university thought us important. I imagined that in the ensuing semesters they would give us teachers of superior caliber—such as our chemistry professor. The very fact that he lectured us for free reinforced my belief.

Analysis would be our first midterm, on a Monday. Since I did not have the textbook I was very worried. I asked the trio whether they would let me study with them over the weekend and they said I could. We would begin on Saturday afternoon. I was less worried when I came to class Friday morning. The night before I had prepared several questions about areas I had not understood so far during the semester. Perhaps Professor Diaz would feel like answering them.

Diaz came in, tall and petulant. "Take out a paper and pencil," he ordered us. He started to write questions on the blackboard. It was the exam!

"But, Professor," someone protested, "the exam doesn't take place until Monday."

"Look, I am the professor here."

"But how can you do this?" The Swiss said. "You yourself told us that it would be on Monday."

"Every one of you has the obligation of learning everything immediately. It is time you know that the university is serious business."

We took the exam as best we could. When we finished we went en masse to the department office. The secretaries did not know what to tell us, it was not their fault, they said. The department chairman, Dr. Kruger, came out to see what was going on. There was nothing he could do, he said. He could not violate Professor Diaz' academic freedom. Then he mentioned that he had a meeting and left.

We went out of the building in a rage, telling engineering students in our path what had happened. That was nothing, we were told. Two years earlier Diaz was teaching a class to a group from architecture. That semester there was a strike just before the final exam. When the strike ended the students returned to take the exam. An hour and a half into the exam some students turned their papers in to Diaz, who began to grade them. He had graded only two when he stood up and hollered at the class to stop writing.

"I've read the first two exams and they are disgusting. I gave them a one. Since I don't want to waste any more time, all of you have a one, too. And let this flunking be a lesson to you about going on strike."

He left the room, leaving everyone astonished. Needless to say, the students made all the trouble they could. The grades were not changed and several flunked out of the university. We also heard that Diaz had ulcers and whenever he had an attack he got even with life by taking it out on the students' grades. Because of his political position, nothing could be done.

The only one who passed in analysis was a detestable redhead who had flunked out of engineering the previous year. I received the second highest grade, but even so I flunked. I passed in all the other midterms, but did really well only in chemistry, in which I got an excellent grade. The Spanish professor had been absent for weeks and he was not about to make a special effort just to give us a midterm.

I felt very depressed. Our group was being treated like any of engineering. At the school it seemed as if the role of the professors was not so much to teach but to eliminate the greatest possible number. In a mathematics or physics section, out of 30 students, only two or three would pass. And of those who passed, very few received truly high grades. One time two Japanese came to teach mathematics. When one of them gave his first midterm the majority of the students passed and several received very good grades. He was fired immediately.

A professor's stature depended on the degree of

difficulty of his classes. And the degree of difficulty of a class was measured by the percentage who flunked. It goes without saying that professors and students hated each other. The students became personal enemies of the professors, and the professors relished flunking them even more.

The pedagogical system was very ingenious: Try to flunk everyone so only the brilliant can graduate. Thus, instead of education, the university practiced Social Darwinism.

Back at home the nagging continued: I was an idiotic dreamer, science was for those who had no stomachs to fill, I would never become a respectable person. One day I responded that it probably made little difference: My father had studied engineering and no one would say he was doing very well. He was furious beyond belief. He at least gave us a decent life, a home, food, an education. (An education?) The majority of people did not even have that. He made so much effort for us, he was killing himself for us. How did I dare treat him as if he were a bum. I was a bad, ungrateful son.

My mother came down, frightened by all the shouting, and then forced me to apologize to my father. The more I delayed my apology, the more offended he was. I finally gave in, but he went on lamenting life's injustice in giving him such a son.

That night I heard him complaining to my mother for hours on end. He ended up by accusing her. It was her fault for treating me as if I were a king, for letting me think that I could do whatever I felt like, for not teaching me to be respectful toward him, for not supporting him sufficiently when I argued back, for...for.... My mother, who had gone along with him at first to calm him down, began to defend herself, and sometimes to defend me, which was further evidence for him that she was on my side and that was the cause of all problems. They ended up shouting at each other. When they finally went to sleep they must have had a very bitter taste in their mouths.

Such fights had become commonplace. And I was the focal point. No matter what the motives—that the money had not lasted long enough that month, that the dinner had not turned out right, that she really wanted to know why he had arrived late on Friday, whatever—in some way the discussion eventually centered on me. She would complain that he treated me very poorly; he that she spoiled me too much and even urged me to be disrespectful toward him.

I, for my part, began to daydream. I made believe that our situation was very different. Sometimes we still lived in Cartagena, in the house in Bocagrande. Or in the mountains of Caldas. And if we did live in Bogota, it was in Santa Ana, in the beautiful house, in the mansion that my father had sold with such unfortunate timing. And that wasn't all, of course. My father behaved as usual, that is, as before. Serious but friendly. Strict but loving. We would still take rides, but not behind the steering wheel of a taxi. And photographs. And we would plan trips, and play soccer or tennis together. And he would surprise us with an invitation to an ice cream parlor, or with money for a game or a movie. And my mother would be teasing, telling stories, playing with the baby, or making sure that the cook fixed us a delicious lunch. If I could again recline on our balcony chairs in Cartagena. Ah. And to let the breeze refresh me and tickle my hair while the sun fell into the sea a mere two blocks away. When night came the lights would go on. Soon my mother would call me to dinner. And on the table there would be a big glass of papaya, curuba, or guanabana *sorbete* to whet my appetite. With mounds of ice. Ah.

That would be my life during my summer vacations from Berkeley or Pasadena, where I would be studying astrophysics and nuclear physics. A nuclear physicist. I imagined modern, beautiful buildings, laboratories that appeared to have been constructed in the future, places where the passion for science was in the very air one breathed. And everything full of light. Light. My real past. My imaginary present. Everything full of light. The opposite of this gray Bogota.

Little by little I ceased paying attention in class. Although, to tell the truth, there was not much worth paying attention to in such classes. Dreams. Light. Light. And I imagined my professors in California: real nuclear physicists. I even gave them names and personalities. And my classmates. Particularly my female classmates. Nude, beautiful bodies close to mine. And ever present a light that cleansed everything, that gave rebirth to everything at every instant, that preserved the world new, vibrant, alive. Alive. Unlike the dirty city that died each day under the dark drizzle.

My disappointment turned into indifference. As if the present did not exist. As if my dreams were reality and all this only a nightmare. I acted in it while waiting...waiting for things to be as they had been, as they should be. As if I were an actor in a bad drama from which I would eventually drop out. But when?

Once in a while I confronted myself. I could not go on like this. I had to do something. But then I would despair. I could not see a way out and would agonize to the point of thinking of suicide. So I would close my eyes and dedicate myself to dreaming. *As Dr. Roberts told me about my projected experiments on sub-atomic particles...it was true that Mary was beautiful...and she loved me so much...how she kissed me in the dark of my room...Mary...Mary....Mary Johnson...or perhaps Mary Brown...*

In the meantime son-of-a-bitch Diaz showed his ineptitude by being unable to explain the limits of a function.

I started to daydream even in chemistry class. The professor's efforts were in vain. To go on working seemed a way of giving myself false hopes. It would be to live a lie.

Instead of living a lie I retired to live in my fantasies. And instead of giving myself false hopes, I dared to believe in changes of fortune more and more incredible each day. I rose early, took the bus, sat in class all day, returned home exhausted, suffered my father's insults and sometimes returned them—without pushing him to the point where he would try to beat me up—and went to sleep...as if it were not me. As if it were all a game in bad taste, a nightmare.

12

In June, when I was supposed to begin my preparations for the final exams, the World Soccer Cup took place in Chile. Since I had neither books nor desire to study I did little but think about the games. What if Colombia pulled off a miracle? Now that the team included Marvel Gamboa anything could happen. But Marvel was injured in the first game, against Uruguay, and Colombia lost 2 - 1.

My attention was drawn to what was going on at the university. The student council organized a big demonstration against the visit of a leading American and the university administration banned the demonstration. There was talk of violence and I decided not to attend classes that day. I would not have gone anyway, for the previous day Colombia had tied Russia in an extraordinary game and I wanted to do nothing but read all the newspapers I could lay my hands on. After being behind by three goals the Colombians took over the field and repeatedly defeated Yashin, the best goalie in the world. Not only did they tie, but they were on the verge of winning the game. The Colombian charge was so spectacular that now everyone was full of hope. It was only a matter of defeating Yugoslavia and our team would qualify for the quarter finals. And since Pele and Diestafano were injured Colombia might be able to beat even Brazil and Spain. I was so absorbed in such daydreaming that I could not even remember the existence of the university.

Unfortunately. The demonstrators attacked the visiting American's car caravan with rocks and hit a little boy's face, shattering his glasses and blinding one of his eyes. The following morning the newspapers produced pictures of the child's face, cut up and bloody, and of his mother, weeping by his side.

The president of the country denounced the "criminal vagrants" who had committed such an atrocity. The university immediately expelled the five directors of the Student Council. No one had to wait for the student leaders' response. A student referendum was called to determine whether we would strike over the expulsion of the five "martyrs." It was understood beforehand that the referendum was a mere formality to give a democratic and legal air to the whole business, for strikes were always approved.

Believing ourselves members of a scarce minority, Alvaro and I voted against the strike. But to everyone's surprise, the motion lost in the referendum. The leaders complained that it was the freshmen students' fault, that we were bourgeois, without social conscience—the "worst" class in dozens of years. So the leaders declared a strike anyway and swore not to let us go to class. Since I did not have the slightest wish to get into trouble, I stayed at home during the days that followed, with my parents' permission. They were afraid that those communist thugs might harm me. I was more interested in the World Cup than in the political question, so I happily stayed in my room listening to the games on the radio.

Alvaro did try to go to class, only to have a girl hit him on the head with a broom. The strikers blocked classroom doors, threw smoke and stink bombs into lectures, let the air out of professors' tires, broke windows, and beat up a few freshmen. The only good thing to come of it was that someone exploded a baloon full of urine on Diaz' face.

While that was happening I was listening to Colombia's decisive game, which ended the way things always end for Colombia: suffering a humiliating rout at the hands (feet?) of Sekularac and the other Yugoslavs. Apparently the game against Russia had been a fluke.

So great was my disappointment that I could not have gone to class anyway. Not even if the things that were going on had not gone on. To end the strike, the administration closed the university indefinitely. According to the communique, once the university reopened, none of the biggest hell-raisers would be readmitted.

Instead of showing satisfaction at forcing the university to close, the strikers proclaimed that it was the duty of all responsible students to make sure that the university remained open. They went so far as begging the professors to return. As they put it, the motive for striking disappeared once the university was closed, since it could no longer serve as a platform. Platform for what? To attack capitalist imperialism. We, the freshmen, laughed at their ridiculous efforts and paid no attention to them.

The unexpected vacation seemed ideal: I could devote myself to the World Cup in Chile. Once Colombia was eliminated Brazil became my favorite. And there were no problems with Brazil. Even without Pele they overwhelmed all their opponents, including the locals (4 - 2), and Czechoslovakia in the final (3 - 1). With the Tellezes and the Millers we did nothing but talk about all the events of the tournament, as we tried to imitate the great heroic deeds of Garrincha, Didi, and company on the concrete of El Polo.

My father told me then that I had to look for a job. Who knows how long the university was going to be closed, he said. I tried explaining to him that the strike had not been my fault, that the university could resume on a moment's notice. He reminded me that I still did not have all my books and that if I wanted them I would have to earn the money. When I replied that I would apparently remain bookless, he was furious and threatened to club me unless I went looking for work the following day.

I did look for work everywhere, as a newsman, salesman, lab assistant, anything. But as soon as I mentioned that I wanted to work only until he strike ended they thanked me for my application and politely ushered me out. After three weeks my father stopped insisting and I stopped looking for work.

The weeks went by slowly, filling me with drowsiness. In my gray room, lying on my green bed, I saturated my mind with Justina, with Consuelo, with Dora. As the paralysis took over my dying willpower, I dreamed of situations in which I took ever increasingly risky action. Ah, if I had searched Justina out. Ah, if I had kissed Consuelo that day. Ah, if I had pulled Dora's panties down. I could still try with the last one. I saw her around the house and we were alone once in a while. But I knew that I would never dare. I had gradually arrived at the point where I observed without participating and day-dreamed without ever planning. If I were studying nuclear physics in the United States...if my father had sent me to California to take the exam for the scholarship...

The University opened two months after the strike began, and a week later we started final exams. Since Alvaro had his mathematics exam the same day I did, and since his book was similar to the one I had not been able to buy, we studied together on the eve of the test. I felt greatly embarrassed by his superior knowledge of the subject. In the exam I did well enough to pass, but barely.

In the perspective geometry final we had two problems, but by the end of the time no one had completed even the first. So the professor told us to finish the other one at home and to turn it in to the secretary on Monday morning. Sunday afternoon I went to Ordonez' house, where he, Lopez, and The Swiss were drawing their answers. When I finished mine Lopez told me that if I had already done the first problem I could give it to him. I did not understand him. Had I not done the first one during the exam? Of course, he explained, but the guys in the class had decided to substitute the ones calmly made at home for those hurriedly drawn in the classroom. The professor had left the first set of drawings in the department office and would pick up the whole thing Monday afternoon.

It wouldn't be hard to fool the secretaries and make the substitution. Lopez and the redhead were in charge. I told him I would not get involved in that scheme. I wonder whether my attitude was the result not of honesty but of fear or laziness.

A few days after the exams ended I went to ask for my grades. The secretary told me that I had flunked two: perspective geometry and mathematical analysis. My knees buckled. I had never failed a subject in my life. To make matters worse, analysis was a prerequisite for the three key subjects of the second semester. So I had practically flunked the entire semester. The secretary must have seen how upset I was for she tried to console me. I should not worry, she said, the whole class had flunked analysis.

"The whole class?"

"Yes, the whole class. Professor Diaz gave everyone a grade between 0.5 and 1.2 in the final."

"But why?"

"That's the way that man is. He probably had one of his ulcer attacks."

"And are they going to let that stand?"

"Oh, no. Dr. Kruger protested to the Dean of

186

Mathematics. They might straighten the matter out."

"How many flunked drafting?"

"Just three."

I was incensed. I had flunked drafting because I had not cheated. And analysis because that son-of-a-bitch Diaz had felt like it. The rest of the day I did nothing but curse Diaz, my classmates, the department, the university, Bogota...

The following day there was a meeting between Kruger and all the students.

The German greeted us nervously and asked us to be silent.

"Well," he said with his heavy accent, "it seems that Professor Diaz left us without any students."

There was laughter.

"The Dean of Mathematics is in agreement with us. The grades are unfair."

Someone applauded.

Now calmer, Kruger continued. "The problem is that it's very hard to change the grades without violating Professor Diaz' academic freedom. It seems that the solution would be to have a committee of three professors grade the exams."

"How long would that take?" The Swiss asked.

"At least two weeks."

"But what do we do in the meantime? The second semester begins in two days," La Tona inquired.

"We have decided that the best way to alleviate the situation is to change from a semester to a yearly program, just for this year. What we are going to do is compute your second semester grades with those of the first and to use the average as your grade for both semesters. So all of you can go on to the second semester."

There was great applause and relieved, happy

cheers. We were saved. Many had flunked three subjects and their careers would have ceased immediately otherwise. I had been rescued by Fate once again. Was it possible for things to really turn out all right? I applauded and laughed with my classmates, for whom I felt friendly camaraderie for the first time.

In very high spirits I walked to Caracas Avenue with The Trio. The second semester I would give my schoolwork all I had, yes sir. Apparently the university considered us very special after all. Next to me, The Swiss was explaining to Lopez how to build a small rocket.

The beginning of the second semester coincided with the September drizzles, and I found myself in the same dark rooms, fighting sleep and cursing the lack of books. This semester I was determined to get ahead. I would adapt to the circumstances. I began to walk with The Trio more often, and not only to walk but to discuss, tease, be a part of the group. Not only with them: I intended to form as many friendships as I could manage. After all, we would be together during several years.

In spite of the new opportunity that the change to an annual program offered, the number of students diminished considerably. On the one hand, many passed the midyear engineering entrance examinations. On the other hand, others were doing so badly that they no longer believed it worthwhile to continue. Through Alba, who had many friends, it was easy to get to know many of my classmates better. A few weeks later, however, my enthusiasm had disappeared. Not only did I find nothing in common with Alba's friends, but I could not stand Alba himself for any prolonged length of time. Apart from his usual boisterousness, now, after his vacations in Girardot, he spent his time telling stories like those of Black Sanchez:

He had fucked his cousins, the police had picked him up at a whorehouse for not paying, and so on. And if the two of them got together it was a fuck-tale tournament.

I was eventually reduced to The Trio, as with the semester before. The Swiss was head of the group. The other two showed near reverence toward him. Ordonez walked by his side, moving his head up and down, always assenting to The Swiss' words. Lopez, always tripping on Ordonez's feet, laughed his servile little laugh. And The Swiss himself, center of all attention, walked as he talked, slowly but firmly. Sometimes we stopped at a store to drink some pop and I could take a look at his face: a strange arrangement of very black eyebrows, blonde hair, and French mouth, as I called it (for as in dubbed foreign movies, the movement of the lips seemed out of synch with the spoken words). The Trio excluded everyone but me, though they never sought my company. I thought about inviting them home to cement the incipient friendship. But I abandoned the idea. ("And who is going to pay for what they eat and drink while they are here?" I could almost hear my father ask.)

Unlike Lopez and Ordonez, I not only argued with The Swiss but even kidded him once in a while. On those occasions Lopez laughed his nervous little laugh (he had many little laughs, Lopez) and The Swiss faked a frown of annoyance. But they treated me cordially and talked about things that interested me.

We also talked about those matters that affected us. In place of Diaz, a fifth year student was teaching us the second course of mathematical analysis (calculus). After the revision of the analysis final exam grades, two of the four of us had now passed and the other two would be in a position to do so at the end of the year. Draftsmanship was the only failure I had to worry about. I would have taken it again immediately, but the class would not be offered until the following semester. The geometry worm had also been replaced. The rest would be the same, except that Kruger was teaching us physics.

My great determination did not last long. Both the calculus professor and Kruger expected us to study the material beforehand. They also required homework every day and we were expected to explain the problems at the blackboard. Since I had no books I could not comply with either of the two requirements. Thus I often made a complete fool of myself at the blackboard. It was my career. My physics. And I, like an idiot, speechless at the blackboard.

My embarrassment was so great, my fear of being called to the board so crippling, that sometimes it was impossible for me to attend either of those two classes. My career. My physics. And I outside, feeling the cold of the city within my soul, watching the gray passing of the endless Bogota hours. As a result I fell behind more and more, and wanted to go to class less and less.

I had no recourse but to ask my father once again, and again.

In vain. He shouted, "'Why didn't you work during the strike?"

"But I looked for a job."

"Two days. Two miserable days."

He ended up insulting me. One day I told him that it would be his fault if I flunked. He slapped my face and left the room.

Whenever I asked my mother for the money, she told me there was nothing she could do. My father was determined. I did not mention the matter again, but my silence must have been very hostile because my father took my mere presence as an accusation and would fight over anything. At night I could hear them argue:

"But he wasn't doing anything," my mother would say.

"Woman, don't I have a right to be the boss in my own house?" he would demand in a loud voice.

And they would take it from there.

"What's the matter with the food?" he would practically shout at me the following evening at dinner. "Isn't it good enough for the dandy?"

"But I haven't said anything."

"Oh, you haven't? Why are you making faces at the food then?"

"I haven't..."

"Oh. Am I a liar then?"

"No, sir."

"If you want to eat better, get a job and pass some money on to your mother."

I decided to remain in my room when we were both in the house, except at dinner time. My absence must have bothered him because one night Dora showed up with his order to go down to the living room.

"Why don't you come down?" my father yelled. "Don't you know that I arrived half an hour ago?"

I remained silent.

"Aren't you going to answer me?"

"I don't know what to say...sir."

"What do you mean you don't know what to say? What about 'Good afternoon, Father,' like a son who respects his father?"

"Good afternoon Father," I said.

He grabbed me by the collar. "Don't make fun of me."

"I wasn't making fun of you," I said, frightened.

"The least you can do is come down to greet me."

And if I did come down he would fight with me for

one reason or another. Dinner time brought another round of insults. He spoke to me with so much wrath that his food probably tasted bitter. And that was on good days. When something did not go well at the office, which was often, he would seek me out in the evening before going to argue with my mother in their room.

I started going to bed early. I did not have much to study anyway, without books. Why does he hate me so much? I asked myself. Perhaps I am not his son after all? Or is he going to lose the job he now has, too? Why did it have to be like that? Perhaps someone would offer him a good position, like the ones he held in earlier years, and his mood would improve. After all, it must be humiliating for a man as capable as he to be working at that job. And for the goverment, on top of it. But why did he have to take it out on me? Oh, if we could return to Bocagrande! If I had left for the United States! And the daydreaming would begin, eventually turning into ordinary dreams ...until my mother's steps on the cold floor woke me in the morning. I would get up shivering, already anticipating the thick, freezing fog that awaited me on the way to the bus.

One time I felt that I was being shaken and I woke up. It was my father. I looked around me. It was still night.

"Get up."

He ordered me to the bathroom. "Look," he said, pointing toward the toilet. It was plugged up.

"It's plugged up," I said.

"And what are you going to do about it?"

"Me? But that's something for the maid."

"The maid has already gone to bed."

"Well. That is none of my concern. Besides, I wasn't the one who plugged it up."

"It is your concern. It's too late to get the maid up and I don't want your mother fixing toilets in the middle of the night."

"I was asleep."

"Sure, since you have nothing to do."

"I didn't plug up the toilet."

"I don't care. You will unplug it, or else I will unplug it with YOU."

And he stayed by the door while I pushed the plunger downwards, on the verge of throwing up.

I could not go back to sleep that night. Goddamn bastard! Why did I continue to defend him in my soliloquies? He deserved what had happened to him. If he found his greatest satisfaction in humiliating me, in showing me his hate, why should I keep myself from hating him, too? I should run away from home. But where? And to what? To clean toilets? Why did I let him do those things to me? Why didn't I stand up to him? Why was I so afraid of him? I felt disgust toward myself, as if I deserved the sour taste of shit in my mouth.

I realized that Homero could not sleep either. I could almost feel his sweaty fists wrathfully closing on the sheets, begging for revenge. He knew what had happened. And my humiliation was his, for the same fate awaited him, very probably. Although not immediately.

In the last few weeks my father had been giving him money to go to parties and the like. To put me down even more, not to please Homero, I suspected. At the parties my brother drank as much as possible in order to come home drunk. Once in a while one of his friends would treat him and my brother would end up with his classmates in a whorehouse. These were his ways of defying my father. But on arriving home he would lose his nerve and fear would sober him up. I stayed up to open the door for him. If my mother or father, especially my father, saw him drunk...why even think about it!

Midterms were coming up and I did not have the calculus and physics books yet. I thought that the best way of solving my problem would be to invite The Trio to study at my house, no matter what my father would say. I asked my mother for permission and she agreed. I now had to convince them. On other occasions I had suggested the same thing, though in a very veiled manner. I had the impression that they thought El Polo was too far away. But this time I was going to invite them directly.

I could not talk to them on the following two days because I was delayed in leaving class and then I could not find them, even though I walked as fast as possible. The third day I was also delayed, talking to the chemistry professor. I decided to take a shortcut to catch up with them on 45th Street. I was practically running when I stumbled upon them. They told me they had gone to the agronomy building and that was why they had not taken their regular route. I was very glad to have found them and asked them right there to study at my place over the weekend. Unfortunately they could not, one had to go somewhere, another had to stay at home; in short, they would each study on his own and whenever possible, though they did not know exactly when.

At the last minute Alba offered me an opportunity to study with him and one of his friends. Since I had no alternative, I accepted. I still liked Alba, though it annoyed me that he resembled Black Sanchez more and more each day. He had picked up the habit of touching other guys all the time. He did it very subtly, and it might have been accidental, but I was suspicious of him.

We met at the engineering library. Just as I feared, Alba began to boast about his conquests. His friend, a guy by the name of Suarez, asked him if it was true that he had fucked his fourteen-year-old boy cousin.

"Yes," Alba began, "I was very bored during the strike and horny as hell. On top of that I didn't even have enough money for cigarettes."

"In Girardot?" the other one asked.

"Yes. You know what that heat is like. It makes you grow horny until you go crazy."

"Why didn't you fuck the maid?"

"The maid is seventy years old and smells like a cadaver. The thing was that my aunt and the boy came to visit us. A beautiful boy. Down there in the hot lands—you have gone to the hot lands, haven't you? Yes...well, in the hot lands, the houses have perforations in the wall, near the ceiling, to circulate the air. The bathroom is that way, too."

"So you were peeping?"

"Of course, thinking that my aunt was going to come in. She's still a pretty young thing. But it was my cousin. To beat his meat, the fucker."

"Did you fuck him right there?"

"No. When he came out I told him that I had seen him and was going to tell his mother. Just to kid him. I wasn't about to rat on him. He started to cry and told me he would do anything I wanted, as long as I didn't tell on him. That's when I got the idea."

"How was it?"

"A lovely ass."

They went on like that. I was simultaneously disgusted and embarrassed, for I had remembered my dream about the Millers.

"Like Ordonez'?" asked Suarez.

I was startled. Were they talking about Ordonez of The Trio? Ordonez with the long legs and the gigantic Goofy feet?

"Yes," Alba said, "very similar. Although the little faces are different."

Ordonez had a "little face"? Were Alba and Suarez pulling my leg? Did they want to shock me?

"The little face of Ordonez is so white," Alba continued, "and that cute, turned-up little nose of his."

"But the best part is the little ass," the other one said.

"Black Sanchez bet me that he will fuck him before the year is out."

I honestly felt sick.

Alba went on, "You know what we should do? We should grab him one of these evenings, after chemistry lab, and take him to some field."

Suarez laughed heartily, showing a great absence of teeth.

All of a sudden they both looked at me, with surprise, as if they had just realized that I was there.

Alba blushed. "We have been joking all along," he told me.

"You finally went too far."

"What do you mean?"

I looked at him with a mixture of disgust and sarcasm.

He flushed. "Look, fucking Martian," he said between his teeth "I'm sick and tired of all your pretensions. If you think you're so superior you don't have to stay with us."

I felt that the situation had changed. Now I was the one being judged. I humbled myself a little: "What pretensions?"

"You put on airs all the time."

"When?"

"Look. Go away."

How dare he? I picked up my notebook. "At least I don't brag about being a faggot."

"Son of a bitch!" he yelled. The few persons in the room turned to look at us, just as Alba stood up to hit me. I felt the blood rushing out of my face. Fortunately Suarez stopped him.

I left then, without having been able to study.

To recover from the incident, once on the bus I gave free rein to my well established social prejudies: I was asking for it by mingling with Southern dwellers, with "Indians." What else could I expect? But presently I sank into the deepest feeling of humiliation, for I remembered the night my father had reduced me to the level of Suarez, of Alba, of Black Sanchez, to the level of the shit that had plugged up the toilet.

13

Chemistry was the first midterm. I did well in it, as usual. I was extremely disgusted by the incredible cheating in the classroom. Papers went from hand to hand, answers were given aloud, exams were compared without any attempt at discretion. Those seated next to me, including The Swiss, were annoyed because I did not let them see my paper. I think the professor realized what was going on but preferred to say nothing.

The cheating gained extraordinary organization in the midterms that followed. Teams were formed, of five to seven students each. The best members sat in the center and solved one problem apiece. The solutions would then be circulated, aided by the department policy that required separate sheets for each answer. Those who contributed less sat on the periphery and received the papers with greater difficulty and for less time, and consequently got the worst grades. A true merit system applied by the students themselves! Great confusion ensued toward the end of every exam, for the smart ones wanted their papers back while the dumb ones wanted to copy longer.

There were a few among us who did not belong to any team. Garcia and I because we were honest. We sat by the window, far from the center of the action. La Tona and the other girl from the South of the city because they were too stupid. No one wanted them near at the time of the exam. The two sat in the middle of the room and tried, begged, and who knows what else, to have something passed their way. The Trio comprised their own group, but since they were few they did not do too well.

In the analysis exam I did well on only two questions. I had to solve two others by combining algebra with the little calculus I knew. Page after page, I developed my own type of solution. I didn't even start the last question. Given the grading habits at the university, I was lost. I did not go to the physics exam the following day. I told Kruger that I had been ill and he let me take it two days later. Since Lopez no longer needed his book he lent it to me. I studied hard until three in the morning and did very well.

When I told The Trio they acted surprised. "You answered all the questions by yourself?" The Swiss inquired.

"Yes.

"How did you manage to copy all the formulas?" Ordonez asked.

"I learned them," I answered.

"You're bullshitting."

"I'm serious. I never cheat."

I was about to tell Ordonez of the conversation between Alba and Sanchez but I contained myself. I would do it on a more propitious occasion. We were presently worried about the exam results.

We found out little by little. I passed in everything, including calculus. The professor must be kind, I thought. After class I saw The Trio arguing among themselves.

"Damnit," The Swiss told Lopez, "I thought you had learned that."

"I thought we had decided not to read it."

"We had decided, yes, but only on Sunday. I thought it was understood that you were going to do it later, on your own."

"After you guys left Sunday night I didn't have any time to study."

By then I was among them. "You guys studied together over the weekend?" I asked them.

Ordonez looked down. The Swiss seemed annoyed.

"Yes," Lopez said. "We decided to get together after all. We would have called you but we didn't know your phone number."

"It didn't do us any good to study, so you are out nothing," The Swiss added.

The only thing left was the written portion of the English exam. The oral portion had been a farce. Every time it was La Tona's turn to read or speak, the professor, short, ugly, and pot-bellied, helped her in a manner that caused either laughter or disgust. "You almost have it, Antonia, you almost have it. That way...very well, very well." And she would go on, pronouncing worse than anybody else, knowing fewer words than anybody else, but getting one of the best grades. "Very well, Antonia." They had been seen together downtown several times, once going into a hotel of ill repute. "You keep improving, Antonia. I am going to give you a four." He tried to trick the rest of us into making mistakes, and then he gave us grades that were as low as they were unfair.

Ordonez was ill and did not take the second part. The exam lasted only forty minutes. The professor collected the papers, shuffled them, and gave them out at random.

"I want you to grade them yourselves. If by chance you end up getting your own, give it back to me and I'll exchange it for another."

He did keep La Tona's exam, certainly, to correct it himself. He gave us instructions and advised us to be honest.

The negotiations between the students began immediately, while the professor graded La Tona's exam.

"Look, I need a four; what if..." "Man, how about raising my grade to three five?" My exam went to Garcia. "You have a three eight," he said. I assented. I could not ask him to raise my grade. He would not do it anyway. I had The Swiss'. A terrible paper. Scarcely a two, and that with some help.

"I need a three five," he told me by gestures.

I moved my head laterally. No. Toward the end he walked by my side. "Damnit, a three at least."

"I'm sorry," I whispered.

After class I saw Lopez and The Swiss walk to 45th Street. I quickened my pace and joined them. The Swiss turned toward me, upset.

"What do you want from me?"

"You shouldn't take it so hard, man. You know I don't cheat."

"You don't cheat, do you?" His face had turned red. "You are so special. So honest. So intelligent. A complete genius. Aren't you? But if you are so perfect, why do you want to join us? So you can brag to us?"

Lopez let out his nervous little laugh.

"What do you mean?" I asked The Swiss.

"You are always following us. Don't you realize we don't like your company? We try to avoid you but you come after us. We even began to walk a different route and you looked for us." He ran out of breath for an instant.

Aha. I now understood many things. How could I have not realized? The feeling of stupidity tripled my embarrassment.

The Swiss continued, "Do you think we have an obligation to listen to you? All the time following us."

He turned his face away and started to walk more quickly. Lopez caught up with him. I kept walking in the same direction, not knowing what else to do. The Swiss must have felt me behind him because he raised his arms to the heavens and yelled at me: "My God! What do you want now?"

"Nothing."

"Why are you following us?"

"I am not following you. Don't I have a right to walk to the bus?"

Lopez laughed loudly. The Swiss' hands remained open, as if imploring. By then we had arrived at 45th Street and I crossed to the other side. We went up to Caracas Avenue that way, the two of them on one sidewalk, Lopez stealing a glimpse at me once in a while, I on the other, returning Lopez's looks.

The city's cold took up residence inside me. It accompanied me in the morning when I caught the bus in the fog, during the day when I endured my classmates' hostility, at night when I ignored my father's insults. Even in my dreams, geometric, sterile, the Bogota cold had intruded, humid, sticky. An icy shell was forming around me, separating me from the rest of the world, making me feel a stranger among my own.

As if I were a Martian. How ironic. The urge to snatch Truth away from a recalcitrant universe seemed not so much foolish as strange—as strange, as incredible, as remote as whatever there was beyond the blackness that crushed the city every night.

I no longer belonged in my home, in my university, in my life. In everything I saw rejection. When I walked on 45th Street toward Caracas Avenue I tried to avoid meeting The Trio, because upon seeing me they changed sides of the street and I felt it like a slap on the face. During the breaks, in the rain, several conversation groups formed, but I was excluded from all of them by a wall of antagonism. So I stood under the portico at the entrance, absorbing the rain's cold, inviting it, offering it a home where it seemed to be so much at ease: inside me.

The beauty of atoms, of supernovas...the light. The light of the galaxies, of the profound prisms of the universe, of my universe. The light in my life. . What foreign yearnings! Like a Martian's. Martian, the one of the grandiose destiny. Bah.

La Tona, who had given me the nickname, now felt justified in avoiding me during the laboratory and shop hours. Since her name followed mine, she had been assigned as my shop partner as well, and, of course, she never helped me. "Who can put up with that conceited Martian?" No, sir. It was not laziness, nor lack of ability, nor even her whoring with the instructors, no, sir: I was so conceited. So she showed up only once in a while, looking very serious in her white robe, to make sure that I was working, for she certainly deserved a good grade and I had no right to deprive her of the fruits of her labor. She would take a glance and go back to flirt with the instructors.

In shop we were doing a unit on electrical motors. La Tona strolled all around the room, but as soon as she saw the supervisor coming she rushed to our motor and sat on the chassis. By the time the supervisor got to our side he found her giving me instructions. "Look, that isn't the way it's supposed to be. The Swiss joined the cables differently. What do you think, Professor?"

Her routine finally irritated me so much that I decided to put an end to it. I disconnected the ground cable and rigged the chassis so La Tona would close the circuit. When I saw her coming I turned the switch on. She started hollering as soon as she sat down. While trying to pry herself loose, she worsened her situation by making more points of contact. I took a second to turn the switch off, but it was enough for her screams to bring half the class running in our direction. When the current ceased she fell to the floor, from where she proceeded to scream as if her crooked teeth were being pulled without anesthesia.

I straightened the wires quickly and no one noticed. The professor took the machine apart to find the cause of the problem. Since he did not find it he gave us another motor and advised La Tona not to sit on it. in the meantime she had settled into a continuous sobbing that did not end until an instructor suggested that she take the rest of the afternoon off. A week later she asked the instructor to let her "work" with some other group because I was very absent-minded. The instructor refused, for it could not have been my fault.

I never knew whether my other classmates suspected me. They thought it was very funny. To the raucous laughter of the group, Black Sanchez imitated La Tona's howling, exaggerating her gestures and interjecting Sanchezisms like "Ouch, they are going to see that I have no underwear on." La Tona found no humor in it and continued accusing me of being stupid and careless.

I kept cutting class. At first out of shame, because without books I could not go prepared. Later out of laziness, or rather, indifference. I didn't care when I was called to the board not having the slightest notion of what to do. Not even my classmates' satisfaction at my ignorance bothered me. Chemistry had also become impossible. The students flew paper airplanes, which sometimes barely missed the professor's head. They laughed, sang—their bad conduct knew no limits. They drank beer in class and even engaged in chalk wars. It was pathetic to see that extraordinary professor trying to ignore the pieces of chalk that flew all over the room. He went on unperturbed, giving his clear, intelligent, interesting, often brilliant explanations—but always pointless and ineffective, always wasted on those future Colombian scientists.

Midterms again. But I could no longer do well. First I flunked physics. Then calculus. The calculus professor asked to speak with me. After class I accompanied him to his office, but before we could talk Garcia joined us.

"Professor," my classmate said, "I must talk to you right now, I can't stand it any longer."

"What's the matter?"

"I flunked once again and it's unfair."

"Do you want me to explain why I graded your exam the way I did?"

"No, it isn't that. I was able to answer only three of the five questions."

"But what do you want me to do? I can't give exams that are any less difficult. I would be fired in the wink of an eye."

"Professor," Garcia had reddened so much that he looked purple, "you know that the way things are, only those who cheat can pass."

The professor looked at him intently. Garcia went on.

"Do you think I'm a fink? Sure, sure, one is not supposed to rat on his classmates, right? Well, I'm sick and tired. You know that everybody cheats. Everybody except Moreira and I. You know it well. The whole world knows it. It's unfair that we flunk and the rest pass."

"I know."

"And why don't you do something? How can it be that the whores get better grades than me? I study...I...La Tona, for example.

The professor interrupted him. "Don't tell me. What for? I know that everybody else cheats, but there is nothing I can do. If I turn anyone in, he would be thrown out of the university. It's far too drastic. And in order to be fair, I would have to turn them all in."

"How can you teach like that?"

"What else can I do? Look, it's worse than you think. La Tona and the other one, for example, copy the formulas on little papers which they fasten on their stockings next to their panties. In the middle of the exam they spread their legs open to read them. Right in front of my eyes. And what do you think they do when they see me? Do they get scared? No. They smile at me, smile at me.... If you want justice or education, go to another country. Nothing can be done here."

"Don't you have an obligation...?"

"To do what? To force the expulsion of the first generation of physicists in Colombia? To tell the truth, the country doesn't need this caliber of scientist. But what do you want me to do? I myself am just a fifth year student."

Garcia walked off in a very bad mood.

"Do you feel the same way?" the professor asked me.

"I don't know. I don't think I care what happens any longer."

"Is that why you flunked my class? Because you no longer care what happens?"

"No. I simply don't have the book."

"Can't you study with somebody else? Or borrow a book?"

"I get along poorly with everyone."

Why did I tell him all these things? As if he were a personal friend.

"What about Garcia?"

"I don't know. I don't know him very well. Maybe I should ask him."

"Do it. And if it doesn't work, why don't you go to

the Engineering Library? You can read calculus books there."

"But it isn't the same."

"Yes, that's a problem. We have nothing but problems. But I didn't order the book. Diaz did. What I would like to do is teach decently, with books in Spanish." He shrugged his shoulders. "Why screw my life up with dreams?"

We had come to the stadium, where he had his office.

"Look, maybe everything is in vain, but I wanted to talk to you. What you did in the first midterm demonstrates that you are a true genius at math."

"But I barely passed!"

"Because you didn't study. Look. Pay attention to me. The way you solved the third problem using algebra, and the other one, not having the foggiest idea of the formulas—that isn't seen very often."

I was very flattered.

He averted his eyes. "Don't let yourself go to waste. Good-bye." He walked away from me with nervous, embarrassed steps.

Garcia never returned to the university. I started going to the Engineering Library, although the books they had were not much help. The order of presentation was different, it was difficult to understand them, and I lacked motivation. I did not miss class anymore, which the professor made easier by not asking me to go to the blackboard. I also went back to physics, to Kruger's frown each time I failed to bring the homework, which was every time.

I greeted no one, I talked to no one, I was interested in no one, and no one was interested in me. Sometimes I tried to understand the situation, but I could not decide whether I had a problem or not.

If it had not been for soccer I would have been devoid of all feeling, of all emotion. What could I care about my classmates' indifference when my friends and I had just entered our own team in a tournament? Soccer had rescued me in one of my worst moments as a stranger, as a Martian. I went to El Campin to watch Millos against Botafogo. To watch Marvel, tall, skinny, black, with his elegance, with his touch, with his blue and white unifom. And the Brazilians. Garrincha, the great Garrincha on the right wing, with his bewitching moves, with those legs of his, one shorter than the other, that wobbled when he walked, that beat the ball when he ran. The great Garrincha, who penetrated any defense, who drove the opponents crazy and the fans wild.

And that was the way the game went. Marvel, impeccable. Garrincha, incredible. Literally phenomenal. Marvel headed in a goal, in a dive from twenty meters out. Precise. Beautiful. Garrincha ran the length of the field, embarrassed the Millos players, came up to the goalkeeper, faked a shot, Centurion dove for it... The ball had not left Garrincha's feet yet! Botafogo's goal. The crowd roared, I as much as anyone. This way I could belong, be alive. This is the way I wanted to live.

By the time I came home I was determined to form a team and to enter it in the Fedenorte's open tournament. The Tellezes, the Millers, and the Moreiras all got together on it. We called it Atletico Pedernal. We wore white pants and gray shirts. It was a unique uniform: no one else sported gray. An elegant gray. Because of it they called us "the aristocrats" later on. Because of it, and because we were the only team in the league composed entirely of people from "good families." Because of the overwhelming presence of "Indians" on the other teams, many friends and acquaintances refused to join. But eventually we recruited enough people, signed up, and bought the uniforms.

We won our first game by routing the opponents, as we would win all our games. We were overpowering in mid-field with our ball control, we dismantled the opposing team and suddenly fired a forward pass to any of our fast strikers. Their goalkeeper would double over in anguish goal after goal. Ah! That was life. The precise pass, the tremendous kick, the goal, the triumph. To feel the blood beating strong in the arteries, from anticipation, from intensity, from struggle, from concentration.

In November everyone went on vacation, except Alvaro and I, since we were at La Nacional. We lost the majority of our players, but still kept on winning, even with only seven players, the seven from El Polo Club. It was almost ridiculous. We all came to the field in just one car, Alvaro's father's. The other teams came in buses, with players to spare and often a large cheering section. They were misled by our number.

Such a great numerical advantage made it easy for them to have possession of the ball most of the time. But in the long run we would take control of the ball and start the rout. There was one game in which we made only five shots on goal. We won five to zero. At the end of the game the goalkeeper sat on the ground and cried.

That feeling of control, of power whenever I intercepted a pass in mid-field and took off with the ball! Forward, to the sides, sometimes fast, sometimes slow, calmly dribbling past opponents, making them fall. And when they cornered me I would cross the ball long, to Ciro or Rodrigo, or would shoot from very far away to the upper angle, by surprise. When the goalie saw the ball it was already inside his goal. I had finally matured as a player. We all had. And we had grown tall and strong, which gave us a great advantage against the small Bogotanians of the other teams. In addition, the many years of playing together bore fruit now: It was as if we had grown a communal sixth sense.

It was like one of my fantasies. Everything perfect. Always in control. Always triumphant. Dribbling, opening up space, passing, moving into the created space, leaping up to head the ball, or for the scissors kick, and falling to the ground, never feeling it, there, on the green grass, next to the small clover, during a very long instant, caressed by the softness of the breeze, as in a dream, as in an underwater swim in a clear lagoon, tense and peaceful at once. There, there, in the long instant after the goal. Before jumping with joy. On the green grass, next to the white line...the tranquility. And then the explosion of the shout of "goal!"

School continued into December and January, but I could care little about what went on. We had midterms again and I flunked physics. I came to the conclusion that I could not pass that class without the book. But how could I ask my father? His efforts to get a good job had proved useless and, to make matters worse, the taxi had given him nothing but headaches and monetary losses. He finally had to sell the damn contraption, which made me glad. But it soured his mood even more. He no longer looked for excuses to quarrel or insult me. He just did it. He was behaving irrationally more frequently, as if the frustration that was eating at his guts had to come out in any way. It occurred to him one day that I should be home by seven every evening. I asked him what I was supposed to do when I had class until seven and he answered that it was my problem; I had a duty to obey him. My mother told him to stop being ridiculous. And the stage was set for a big fight.

The following night I came home at eleven. He was waiting for me, belt in hand. Fortunately my mother came down the stairs when she heard his hollering and mine, and prevented his hitting me. He started shouting at her that his sons' lack of respect toward him was her fault.

"What respect can they have toward you," my mother answered, "when you conduct yourself in this manner? Respect must be earned."

"Oh. So I haven't earned it!"

"No. You have no right to treat your sons like slaves."

"Then you think it's fine for them to be out on the street until whatever hour of the night they see fit. You," he addressed me, "what business do you have outside at this time?"

"I..."

"It doesn't make any difference," my mother interjected, "you well know that Oscar has no vices. So what harm could he be doing? Besides, he is a college student; you can't keep treating him as if he were a little boy."

"If he is such a grown-up, why doesn't he get a job to help us? He could at least help himself."

My mother told him to stop being an imbecile, and they went on arguing for a long while. Things of that sort happened almost every day. How could I ask him for the book? I explained the situation to my mother. That night they had a big confrontation about it. My mother threatened him with asking her father for the money and my father shouted that she could do whatever she felt like.

He did not believe that my mother would dare

"humiliate" him like that. So he was enormously surprised when my grandfather's letter came with a check for
my physics book. From then on he stopped talking to me.
Not only that, he also refused to eat if I was in the dining
room. Since the tension at the table was so disagreeable,
with his standing up to leave whenever I came in, or his
refusing to sit down if I was already there, I asked my
mother if I could be served in my room. But then when he
saw the maid go up the stairs with my food he complained
about how my mother spoiled me.

14

The great games of Atletico Pedernal continued. The other members returned in February and the team was back at full strength. By then all the other teams knew of us. Some of them played us with so much fear that they practically gave the game away beforehand. Week after week went by, fuzzy bridges between soccer weekends. Pedernal and Millonarios. In my daydreams I changed the uniform colors: blue instead of gray. I saw myself as inside right for Millonarios, taking over the ball, controlling the field, making the spectacular pass, striking the ball furiously. And blue again as inside right for a victorious Colombian National team.

And who would be the future stars? The ones from Pedernal, of course. Homero, and Carlos, and Rodrigo, and the Tellezes, and.... Sometimes I told them that if we kept improving we would get to be professionals. They found that amusing. After all, we were only playing in a Fedenorte tournament. But this time it would work out. Something had to come out all right for me.

I had resolved to study diligently but at the hour of truth I found myself paralyzed in my gray room. My mind simply slid over the covers of the books, lost in a torpor from which I came out only to answer Homero's questions. My brother was preparing for the admission exams. ("At La Nacional, Father, of course.") He was going to win the scholarship I had wasted. At last, another Moreira engineer.

It was strange that we had never talked about the university, about physics. It would have been natural for him to aspire to be a nuclear physicist or an astrophysicist. But since my entrance to La Nacional our discussions about the future, about the nature of the universe, about the possibility of extraterrestial life had diminished almost to the point of disappearing. We no longer even read the glossy black paperbacks. My disappointment became his resignation. How many of his drunken sprees had been because of me?

My brother passed his exams and felt content. My mother, happy. My father, relieved. He had feared that Homero might perpetrate the same ignominy. No. He would be a true Moreira.

My father's silence toward me became still more impenetrable.

In the meantime I had passed the calculus exam. I had only English and physics left. I finally had the physics textbook. But I could not study. I spent whole days lying on my bed, balancing the thick book on my knees. I took the English exam. The physics book remained closed a couple of days more. Such an incredible fight with my father over the damn book and I was not going to use it?

I began to study three days before the exam. Midnight came. Homero returned from one of his many celebrations. He went to sleep. I studied, concentrated through the small hours of the night. Concentration. As in the fourth of secondary. Even before then. When I was allegedly promising.

The shout straightened me in my chair. I thought I had been dreaming. But it was not a dream. Homero had been awakened by it, too. The baby started crying. Another shout by my mother pierced our nerves. And then came the anguished sobbing. We ran toward my parents' bedroom. "My God," I heard Homero mutter.

Their door opened suddenly and the startling light stopped us in the semi-darkness of the hallway. My mother crossed the doorway, crying, about to fall.

"What's the matter?" Homero yelled, frightened.

"Your father!"

"What?"

She sobbed again. I looked at her eyes and the pain I saw there made me lower mine, confused.

"Dead. He's dead."

I heard Dora cry out, behind me. Baby Ruben screamed in panic, in his bed, not knowing what was going on. Homero went by my mother and entered the room. She sat on the stairs and Dora ran to her, to hug her, to share her torn, hysterical weeping. After a while, a long while, Homero returned with Ruben. The little one clung to my mother's neck. Homero knelt next to her. "Mother, oh, mother," he cried.

I just looked at the four of them for a long time, not knowing what to say.

The ringing of the doorbell shook us. Homero went down to see who it was. The disturbance had awakened the neighbors. My brother explained what had happened. The voices arrived, strange sounds to us now, bringing in the night cold. The baby and Dora kept quiet. My mother went on sobbing. I could not move. They were giving Homero their condolences when we heard other voices. It was Alvaro and Benito Tellez.

Alvaro came up the stairs. "Mrs. Moreira," he said to my mother. "I am very sorry."

"Thanks, Alvaro."

My friend stroked the baby's head for a second,

and then stood in front of me. I remained in the same place, stunned.

"Oscar..."

I lowered my eyes. He put his hand on my shoulder. Homero came up behind Benito. There was another round of condolences. The three of them went into my parents' bedroom. I wanted to follow them but I could not move.

Alvaro returned, very pale, to speak with my mother. He wanted to know whether we had called anyone. She answered that we hadn't. Alvaro went down to phone my grandparents and the doctor. Benito and Homero helped my mother and Dora to my sister's room. The baby followed them. I remained in the same place, like a statue in pajamas. Ciro and his mother found me there when they came up. A while later Mrs. Tellez took some clothes out of my parents' room for my mother. Homero told me to get dressed and I finally came out of my immobility.

The doctor came rushing in, followed a few minutes later by my grandparents. The wailing and weeping began anew. I was the only one who had not cried and that made me feel guilty. It was my father. My father had just died. Didn't I care? I tried to let the magnitude of the event enter me, take hold of me, overwhelm me with pain. But nothing. I was cold. Empty. I could no longer respond. I lowered my eyes once again. I did not want anyone to see my lack of sorrow.

"A heart attack," someone said.

The bell rang again. It was the Millers. Carlos and Rodrigo embraced all the Moreiras. Mrs. Tellez had fixed coffee and chocolate and her sons were serving it. The whispers spread throughout the house. "A heart attack."

The men from the mortuary came early in the morning to take my father's body away. They brought it back that afternoon, in an enormous black coffin, which they placed between four candles in the middle of the living room. "Don't worry about the burial," my grandfather had told my mother. During the day one of my uncles bought us black clothing. Dora could not stop crying. Homero would let his eyes fill with tears before drying them. I lowered my eyes, pressed my lips together and tried to appear mournful. I wanted to give the impression that only my maturity kept me from crying.

Aunts and uncles, friends of the family, employees in my father's office, and neighbors paraded through our living room. There was a small crowd of maids and neighborhood children outside. Every once in a while the man from the flower shop arrived with more flowers whose scent became overpowering in our small and dark living room.

My mother and my grandparents sat on a sofa at the entrance to the living room. We children spent our time on the other sofa. A visitor would come, he would offer his condolences, they would offer him a chair, he would have a cup of coffee...

"And still so young."

"At the peak of his life."

"The will of God."

"The Lord knows his own ways."

I felt like arguing, saying that if there was a God, this seemed to be the only thing he was good for. But my mother would have been insulted. Couldn't I respect my father's memory? Did I perhaps hate him? She who had always taken my side.... Why did she not talk to me? Why did she not look at me? Did she think I was in any way at fault? Or did she feel guilty because of me?

I straightened my sailor's hat. The motorboat cut a wave in two. Bocachica Beach could be seen clearly already. I looked back. Instead of receding, Cartagena seemed to extend, to embrace us on all sides. The petrochemical company boat reduced speed. A ship appeared to the north. "Is that a destroyer?" my father asked the boat's pilot. "Yes, Doctor." Dora was sitting next to my mother. "Mother," my sister asked, "how come emeralds are green and not blue?" I smiled. I looked at my father. He smiled, too. We exchanged another smile, of understanding. "If they were blue they would be like this sea," my mother said.

Homero stood up to observe the body in the coffin. He sat down again. "He looks as if he were just asleep," he said. I had not seen my father dead. I did not want to see him. I said nothing.

In the evening we went to the Tellezes for dinner. First the children. Then my mother and my grandparents. The Tellezes, whose father was dying of cancer in the hospital, knew what to do, what to say. Alvaro placed himself in charge of everything, as if it were his duty. He advised us to take a nap, for the wake would last all night. Only Dora and the baby followed his advice.

The little model airplane gained altitude, the wind shook it, threw it against the branches of a eucalyptus. Homero and I ran to the tree. My father came up beside us. "Is it broken?" "I don't know," I told him. "It's between the leaves and we can't see it well." "Why don't you bring it down?" "It's too high." He then grabbed me by the waist and helped me climb. I took the model airplane and passed it to him carefully. "It just has a broken wing," he said. "It won't be hard to fix it."

My maternal grandfather arrived about eight. He had just flown in from Cali. There was a fresh round of tears.

"You can't play badminton here in Caldas," my father said, putting the racket down on the ground. "It's too windy."

Two dark figures crossed the threshold. Father Jorge and the rector. They had found out through Rodrigo Miller. I was surprised. My mother was extremely grateful. "I can't thank you enough, Father. So good of you to remember us...." She was talking to the rector. "Two of our best students," he was saying. Father Jorge put his hands on my shoulders. "Oscar, you have to help your mother." "Yes, Father." They stayed about fifteen minutes. Abelardo Garcia called from Belencito. Would Consuelo be near him just then?

At nine my uncle Fabio walked in with his wife and daughters.

"We came right away," he told my mother.

My cousins had grown. Inez had become a polished young woman. Later on she told us that her boyfriend had already talked to her about marriage. Ester was now a beautiful blue-eyed blonde with magnificent breasts. I did not miss the look that Rodrigo Miller threw her way. My cousin was the quiet type, however, and apparently ill-tempered. She frowned all night long. She seemed very ill at ease.

We had not seen them since those vacations in Cartagena. Cartagena. Where we had been happy. My father had promised to send me abroad. I felt sleepy. Now he was in that box, dead, after his long, hateful silence.

Dead. Damn Bogota. The sea breeze.... Now it could never be again. He had gone without our being able to understand each other again. He had gone full of resentment. As if there had been only Bogota. As if Cartagena and Caldas had never been. Dreams...dreams...he would never come back. The beach in Bocagrande...had all that existed? I hadn't invented it? Wasn't everything gray, dark? Wasn't that the way it had to be? Dreams...Bocagrande...The backyard...Justina against the trunk of the papaya tree...my uncle Fabio.... But no. It was not Justina. It was my cousin Ester. The hair blonde, not red like Justina's. Against the trunk of the papaya tree...naked, blonde pubic hair...enormous tits...and my uncle Fabio: "Come, darling, I'll show you how much I love you." My cousin's hips, stiff, against the trunk...her face stiff, bored....and my uncle laughing boisterously....

Someone sat on the sofa and the movement awakened me. My uncle Fabio was talking to his father. My maternal grandfather did not seem to be paying attention to him. My cousin Ester was still frowning. What a ridiculous dream! I felt an urge to laugh. I contained myself. I became fearful that I might begin laughing uncontrollably, hysterically, at any moment. Everyone would look at me accusingly: "Aha! He hated his father. Look how funny he thinks it is." And the more I dreaded it, the greater my urge to laugh.

I went up to the bathroom. Closed the door. Made faces at my reflection in the mirror to relieve my urge to laugh. Turned on the faucet and laughed a little bit, quietly. I forced myself to stop. The lower ribs began to hurt, as if someone were tickling me. Tickles. Someone should tickle Ester. Naked. Against the trunk of the papaya tree.

I lowered my pants. Sat on the toilet seat. Beat off. When I finished I thought about Father Jorge. Fa-

220

ther, it was only a filthy thought. I laughed. Made more faces at the mirror.

The burial took place early in the morning. We first attended a long mass during which the organ tortured my ears and the heavy smell of incense brought me to the verge of vomiting. Then came the procession to the cemetery. The speech by one of my father's friends (the one who had talked him into buying the distributing house) in front of the Moreira mausoleum: "Our shared sorrow...proud of having been his friend...great future..." Then it was the priest's turn. They were about to put my father in that hole in the wall. Couldn't I feel anything? The trips all over the country, the motorboat in Cartagena, the model airplanes in Caldas...My father. My father. Not even a tear? And what would have been our life? Buying the house in Bocagrande, a few steps from the beach. Going to study abroad. Nuclear physics. Coming back for vacation. To play tennis and chess with him. To talk about his plans and mine. Upstairs, on the balcony, when the breeze arrived with the moon and the crickets. While we waited for dinner to be served. Ah. Cartagena. Cal Tech. A true city. True nuclear physics. A true father. Smiling. Alive. Alive. Unlike the one they were about to put in that hole that smelled of fresh cement.

No one cried. My mother closed her eyes. Dora hugged the baby. My grandfather, tall like my father, though now slightly stooped, gave the signal. The hole, Bogotanian, disgusting, swallowed up my father's body.

Once again I felt the urge to laugh. If only I could cry instead. I realized that I did not hate him. No. No death would have made me cry. Not even my mother's, nor Homero's. Nothing would have made me cry. The thought horrified me. Or, rather, I believed that it should horrify me. I could not feel anything. It was as if the city had placed me in the coffin with my father.

The following morning I took the physics exam. I did not want to fail the subject, for I would fall behind a semester. As it was, I would have to take the draftsmanship class over. Kruger came into the room and wrote the questions on the board. There were seven problems. I studied them carefully. Near me, the cheating began immediately. I could answer three at best—there was no way for me to pass. I wrote my name on the piece of paper. Crossed it out. I stood up, picked up the ballpoint pen, walked to the door.

Kruger caught up with me at the doorway.

"Where are you going? I haven't given you permission to leave."

"Anywhere. To a movie."

"A movie? What are you talking about? What movie?"

"A French movie."

"Have you gone mad?"

I shrugged my shoulders and started walking. Kruger followed me a couple of steps. "Come back!"

I did not even turn my head.

We played our last game of the tournament that Sunday. The opposing team had lost only one game, so if we lost they would tie us in the standings. All our players wore a black band on their left arms, as a sign of mourning for my father.

A few minutes into the game we scored a goal. It seemed a game like all the rest. But little by little they began to take over. Our goalkeeper was distracted and they tied with a long shot. I became nervous. I started to lose the ball, to make bad passes, to play poorly. In the first minute of the second half they scored another goal. They continued to control the game. I couldn't allow us to lose. Their left wing had the ball in our territory. I pursued him to the corner, hustled him, took the ball away from him and passed it to Benito. Benito passed it forward to me and I touched it to Alvaro. Alvaro gave it back to me. I dribbled past two opponents. Ciro came to help me. In a "wall" play we eluded two more. All of a sudden I found myself in front of the goal, running as never before. I put all my weight on my right leg in a furious kick. But the ball had fallen in a dip and I kicked the air. My whole body crushed my knee against the ground.

The world was obscured by a fog of cold sweat. I felt hands picking me up and carrying me. When I came to I found myself off the field, attended by Alvaro, Carlos and Homero.

"Your knee is badly injured," Alvaro told me. "I think I should take you to a hospital."

I told him to finish the game, that it didn't hurt all that much.

A cousin of the Tellezes took my place. I tried to move but the pain prevented me. Our opponents made another goal. They embraced happily. The fans called them champions, chanted for another goal.

But suddenly our team started to move. In less than five minutes we scored four goals. The opponents were completely deflated and practically disappeared from the field. Toward the end we scored two more goals. We were champions.

If it had not been for the intense pain, I would have joined the rest in our victory dance. The league president came to congratulate me, since I was the captain.

Smiling and groaning, I was taken to the hospital

by Alvaro.

My mother almost fainted when I came home on crutches. Alvaro told her that I would be alright in a couple of weeks and she calmed down a bit.

"You should be more careful, Oscar. What will I do if something happens to you?"

My mother looked so old. And only three and a half years had passed since our arrival at El Polo Club.

I went back to see the doctor. He told me that I had water on the knee. It would be better for me to not play soccer for a couple of years.

"And then?"

"It would be better for you not to. But if you do, be very careful."

I felt that soccer was going out of my life. As everything else.

I could still go to the stadium to watch Millonarios play. But now that the possibility of ever seeing myself on that field was gone, it was not the same.

There was a ceremony at the Fedenorte. All our players attended it. Since I was on crutches, Alvaro went up to the stage to receive the trophy. Afterwards we congratulated one another, and the others talked about entering the regular tournament. The only obstacle was the high entry fee. Nothing was decided, however.

Upon my father's death my family was left practically in poverty. Thanks to the insurance, the house was completely ours. But if we did not rent it we would have no means of eating. And if we rented it we would have to move to a cheaper place, to a place worse than El Polo. I imagined from time to time that I would have to go to work, though I did not know what kind of job I could possibly get. Just a year earlier such a matter would have worried me exceedingly, but I could scarcely concern myself over it now. Seeing that the days were passing, I urged myself to solve the problem. Since I was the eldest son I should take the responsibility of planning for the future, at least of discussing the situation with my mother. But I postponed even thinking about it. I told myself that I had enough with the pain in my knee, with the uncomfortable crutches, with everything.

I was lying in bed one afternoon, "resting," when my mother came in. She sat on the edge of homero's bed. Her eyes were as sad as her black dress, her mouth so exhausted that it seemed permanently parted from crying.

"You'll be going back to classes next week."

"Yes, Mother."

"And so will Homero.

"I looked at her with impatience. Waiting for her to get to the point.

"I hope you won't need the crutches."

"I can nearly walk without them."

We remained in silence for a few minutes. Was she going to talk about my father? About my father's silence? About why he treated me so poorly? About why we had to forgive? About why it had not been my fault, nor hers? About that being the way life was? God's will? About my having to go to work so Dora and the baby would not starve?

"I've been talking with my father and with Fabio," she finally said.

"Oh?"

"They are both going to move away from Manizales. Your uncle Fabio is coming to Bogota and your grandfather is going to Cartagena."

"What is the old man going to do by himself in Cartagena? Wasn't he supposed to have retired?"

"He likes Cartagena. And he has several friends there. He's even going to buy a house in Bocagrande. Besides...he isn't going there by himself."

"How so?"

"He asked us to live with him and I accepted. He's going to pay for all the house expenses plus Dora's and the baby's education. With that and the money from the rent we will have enough. There's nothing to be worried about where Homero is concerned, because he has his scholarship."

I was the only one left out. "And what do I do? Get myself a little job?"

She resented my words. "Don't do that to me. You know how important I think your education is. Otherwise..." She paused. A tear peeked out of her eye. "Your Uncle Fabio has offered to have the two of you live at his home."

"Out of charity?"

She was very annoyed. "Not out of charity. Because he is your uncle and he is fond of you."

There was a long pause.

"They are going to rent a house just a few blocks from the university."

Since I was still on crutches, Homero took care of moving my things to Uncle Fabio's house. The Tellezes and the Millers helped with the furniture. Afterwards they all returned to help my mother pack for Cartagena.

They were finished in a few hours. A truck came toward evening to pick up everything but the suitcases. Night fell. Dark shadows filled the house, almost empty, almost naked. I went into my room for the last time. What was left for me in it? Memories that would make me cry, that would make me laugh? Hopes? Dreams that would make me feel? I found only a small and ugly room. I turned out the light and closed the door.

15

Uncle Fabio's house was large, modern, comfortable, and full of color. The opposite of the one in El Polo. They gave Homero and me an ample room with large windows that looked onto the street.

It was next to my cousin Ester's room. "Aha!" Rodrigo said, a suspicious smile on his face, when I told him. Since I did not respond, he added, "You're a sleepwalker, aren't you?" I invited him to visit me as often as he wanted.

Unfortunately my cousin seemed to dislike me strongly from the start. She avoided me, would not answer my questions unless her parents were present, and then only to keep from being scolded by them. Sometimes, when she saw me limping (I was no longer on crutches), she betrayed a mocking expression.

The first Sunday morning she came to tell me that the car was ready to go to church. She had obviously been sent to do it, for she did not seem pleased.

"I don't go to church."

My answer surprised her. "How come?"

"I'm an atheist."

She looked me over intently for a moment, then shrugged her shoulders and went off. She despised me, and her contempt was humiliating. I should teach her a lesson. Those beautiful tits. I should grab them and squeeze until she cried in pain. She would stop looking at me as if I were a worm. But no, she would probably spit on my face. And what would my uncle and aunt say when she accused me, full of indignation and hate?

My relations with the rest of the household were cordial, but not excessively so. It seemed to me that they found me a bit strange. (A Martian? I asked myself.)

Homero, on the contrary, got along very well with everyone. Thanks to him, my cousins, who knew no one in Bogota, were invited to a large number of parties and picnics. With them, it was Homero this and Homero that. My aunt and uncle were also very fond of him and spoke of how good-looking, polite, and pleasant he was. My brother loved the attention. After some time I realized that he was a bit embarrassed by my "peculiarity," as if he had to apologize for me to my cousins.

The day of registration I went to the department office to do the paperwork. On the way there I felt irritated. My knee was still hurting, for one thing. I cursed my lack of effort in physics, for another. If I had received at least a two, I might have passed the habilitation exam (a regularly scheduled exam taken after failing a course; a passing grade in it substitutes for the course grade). If I had earned the right to that second chance I would have studied like mad then, and perhaps.... Why lie to myself? I thought. I would not have studied. Now I had to take the subject over. That and draftsmanship as well.

When I asked the secretary for instructions she looked surprised.

"But you flunked out. You can't take classes here."

"What? What are you talking about?"

"Moreira, right? Here it is. Three subjects failed."

"Three subjects? Which three?"

"Draftsmanship, physics, and mathematical analysis."

"Analysis? But the calculus professor told me that I had passed."

"It's written here."

"He told me so himself!"

"Let me see. That's right. You passed calculus but you got a one the first semester. Since the two grades are computed together, you end up with a 2.2."

"How come? After they revised my first semester exam, I was told that I had passed that subject as well."

"It was decided that the grades given by Professor Diaz couldn't be changed."

"But why not?"

"Because of the constitutional charter of the university."

"What are you talking about? This is a rotten thing to do!"

"Why didn't you take the habilitation exam?"

"How was I supposed to know?"

"How did the others know?"

"You can't get away with this!"

"What do you want me to do? I'm only the secretary."

"I want to talk to Kruger."

"Doctor Kruger is very busy."

She turned away and started typing. I remained in the same spot, staring at her face, which must have irritated her, for she stopped typing.

"What is it now?"

"I want to see Kruger. Doctor Kruger."

She sighed with exasperation. "All right, I'll tell him."

She came back a few minutes later. "Doctor Kruger will see you in half an hour."

I sat down to wait. I heard loud laughter in the hallway. It had to be Alba. I hoped he would not come into the department's office. I did not want to see any of my classmates. But when he went by the door he saw me and came in. He was friendly and that surprised me. He sat by my side. "So they fucked you up, too, didn't they?" he asked.

"What do you mean?"

"The analysis business."

"Ah. You, too, Alba?"

"Yes.

"They are a bunch of sons of bitches." The secretary heard me and gave me a nasty look. "And bitches," I added. The secretary stopped looking at me. Alba laughed noisily.

"Do you know why they did it?"

"I'm not sure. Something about the university constitution."

"That's a pile of shit. The truth is that too many passed on to the second year. So they decided to let Diaz' grades stand, to reduce the number of students."

"Did you flunk out, too?"

"Yes, I flunked physics, geometry, English, and analysis. I was lost, no matter what."

Black Sanchez walked by in the hallway and Alba went after him. A while later the secretary let me in to see Kruger, who received me coldly. I reminded him of the promise he had made six months earlier about straightening out the analysis business.

That annoyed him. "Yes, yes," he said impatiently, "but it wasn't possible. Professor Diaz' academic freedom couldn't be violated."

"But how can you let the students be abused like that? How...?"

"Look," he cut me short, "You flunked three subjects. No good student has been harmed."

How could I tell him that I was a good student? I felt lost. "Doctor Kruger, we agreed to change to a yearly program because it was supposed to favor us. But the way you are interpreting things, we come out at a disadvantage."

"I didn't handle the problem of that subject by myself."

"I'm not talking about analysis anymore. Listen, if the program hadn't been changed, at the end of the first semester I would have flunked two subjects. I would've still remained in the department. In the second semester I flunked only one. With the change of program you count them as three in one term and I'm out of the department."

"Is that the opinion of the other students?" He looked at me with undisguised sarcasm: "Perhaps your former classmates will want to support you."

I swallowed back the insults I wanted to shout at him. I composed myself and proceeded: "If the department had offered a draftsmanship class during the second semester I would have had only two failing grades at the end of the year."

"We couldn't offer a freshman class for only three students."

"But that wasn't my fault. Besides, don't you think that if I know calculus I know the necessary mathematics to go on? Don't you think it's unfair for me to flunk out like that?"

"If you knew so much mathematics, why didn't you take the habilitation exam?"

"The calculus professor told me that I had passed in his class. What was I supposed to do then? How could I know that you had not kept your word in the Diaz matter?"

"In the first place we didn't give you our word." Kruger was furious. "In the second place, you could have asked for your grades at the department's office."

"But I believed that I had passed!"

"You believed! Did you also believe that the university is a game? Don't you have any sense of responsibility?"

I felt consternation. "What am I going to do now?" I immediately regretted having asked such a thing.

He looked at me intently. "Why don't you go to a movie?" He smiled at me. "To a French movie."

I came out of the department's office almost running, the pain in my knee notwithstanding, looking for a place where I could let flow the tears that would certainly gush to my eyes. I went into a grove of trees and sat on a bench, ready to vent my feelings.

But nothing happened. My eyes were dry. I was surprised. It was as if nothing had happened. But how could that be? They had just kicked me out of the university. There was no longer even the possibility that things might change some day, that I might have better professors, that my career would turn into real science. How was it possible for me not to feel pain, anguish, even despair? And they had kicked me out with tricks, with deceit. Why wasn't I outraged? Was I empty? Dead? Why couldn't I cry? Why didn't I feel like crying?

My passion, my great passion had been to discover the nature of the universe, my place in it, to be able to understand...understand everything. Didn't I care about anything anymore? How could that be?

The one chosen by Destiny! The master of fate! Life had gone one way and I another, daydreaming. My father was buried. Things would never be straightened out between us. My knee was injured. I would never be able to realize my soccer ambitions. I couldn't even play. I no longer had a career, no matter how bad the university had been. I would never be able to answer the great questions. Not even ask them well. What was I going to do?

Kicked out of the university! That was my ultimate defeat. What had happened to me? Before, I had wanted to understand everything. Everything. The great questions about the universe. Now it was imperative for me to answer at least my own question: What had happened to me? I had to understand that. I did not want to go on unable to cry.

I also had to tell my mother, Romero, Uncle Fabio. And then my friends. But I postponed the disagreeable task a few days, which turned into a few weeks. Since I could not stay home all day long without arousing suspicion, I went out every morning with a notebook in my hand. I then started walking, in any direction. Until the pain in my knee kept me from going on. I would rest a while and then turn back. When my knee stopped hurting my walks became endless. Sometimes I had to take a bus to make it home in time for dinner.

I walked with the rhythm of the city. People came and went, talked, laughed, hurried to take buses and taxis, to beat the traffic lights. And the city went on, marching through the inexhaustible minutes of the day. The gray indifference of the sky would turn black and it would rain with exasperating boredom. People would run to escape the downpour, to wait until they could proceed with their lives.

In my first walks I would put the notebook on my head to protect myself a little from the rain. But I soon stopped taking precautions. The water soaked my clothes, made them stick to my body, chilled my bones. Once in a while, a shiver would interrupt the flow of my thoughts and I would welcome it: It was pleasant to feel something.

I had to understand. Understand. Review everything that had happened to me since our arrival in Bogota.

Perhaps then I would find the key. The city had swallowed my soul, I told myself by Caracas Avenue and 50th Street; it was the city's fault, I assured myself on 72nd Street.

Damn Bogota. I could not even go back to Cartagena anymore, not to live, no. Neither to Cartagena nor anywhere else. There would not be new places full of light and green. Because I carried Bogota inside me. And the people kept running to escape the rain, to catch a bus...

I could not go back to Cartagena. How could I? No longer with feelings, no longer with dreams, no longer with my father...no longer with my father. Bogota had destroyed my father. It had devoured him. The multitude continued talking, laughing, crying by my side, as in a movie, except that I was the one who moved. Talking, laughing, crying. And I could not talk, laugh, cry with them.

I sometimes imagined that everyone around me was an actor, that all feeling and emotion had disappeared from the planet but no one wanted to admit it.

Why did I have to be different? I began to play-act: I was a madman, a Martian. No, a man full of self-pity. No, rather, a misunderstood genius. But the theater did not help me. And I ended up alone. Alone in the streets of Bogota. Alone in my room while Homero studied, entertained friends, went to parties, or chatted with my aunt and cousins.

Alone all week long. But then came Sunday and I went to the stadium, to shout, to insult, to cheer with the crowd. To live, one day out of the week. To live as a spectator.

I started walking at night, too. And while walking, I recounted my own story. The story that only I could care about.

When I returned home one Saturday night, I found my cousin Ester in her baby doll pajamas, reclining on the sofa of the dimly lit living room. I let myself fall on a chair in front of her, at once hoping and fearing that she would leave.

"You look tired," she said.

"I am."

"Where were you?"

"Out walking."

"Walking? The rest of the world goes to parties or to the movies. You walk."

"I walk."

Those enormous golden tits, scarcely disguised by the cloth. Those bare legs. That blonde hair. The woman of my dreams, my Diana. I wanted to come close to her, to touch her, to kiss her. To talk to her about what was happening to me. To kiss her.

"And what about you? What are you doing here on a Saturday night? Weren't you all supposed to go to a party?"

"Everybody else went, but I stayed because I wasn't feeling well."

"Are you feeling better now?"

"Yes, thank you." She smiled at me. Those lips.

A pleasant silence came upon the living room. I smiled at her.

Perhaps I should get close to her, I thought. But all of a sudden she yawned. Was she bored?

"Are you going to the game tomorrow?"

"Like every Sunday. I even go when Santa Fe is the one playing."

"Would you like to play?"

"What?"

"Be a professional player."

"Of course."

"I can't understand that."

"Why not?"

"Because only the sons of laborers get into those things. I can't understand why a boy from a decent family..." She yawned once more.

"Soccer is an art. It makes one alive, besides, and..."

She stood up suddenly. "Good night," she said and left, leaving me in midsentence. She went up the stairs and slammed the door after her, so I should have the certainty that she wanted nothing to do with me that night, any night.

My night walks became longer. I started returning after midnight. I once met my uncle at the front door.

"How are you, Uncle?"

"Ssh."

He opened the door and we went in.

"You also have some business to take care of until late, don't you?" he whispered. He was drunk. "No, schoolwork, schoolwork. Ha, ha."

Later, in my room, it occurred to me that perhaps Justina was living in Bogota.

My body at long last could not put up with all those walks in the rain and I fell ill, which gave me a perfect excuse to stay in bed several days.

One morning I felt someone shaking me rudely. I opened my eyes. It was Homero. He wore an expression I had never seen on him: He seemed about to cry from sorrow and anger at the same time.

"What's the matter?" I asked him.

"I know."

"What?"

"That you're a hypocrite. A liar."

I sat up in bed. "What are you talking about?"

"The Swiss told me."

A shiver ran through my body.

"The Swiss?"

"Yes, The Swiss. Don't be an asshole."

"How do you know The Swiss?"

"Goddamnit! What does that matter? What matters is that he told me. I've just come from the physics department. You flunked out."

"No."

"What do you mean, 'no'? Don't give me any bullshit."

"I didn't flunk out. It was a rotten thing they did to me."

"Oh, sure. And in the meantime you pretended to go to school. A complete sponger. And a liar. What is Uncle Fabio going to say?"

"He can say whatever he feels like."

"So you're ungrateful as well. As if he hasn't been supporting you all this time."

"You are absolutely right. Poor uncle, I shouldn't have taken the bread out of his mouth."

"Go on. Go on. And what are you going to tell our mother? As if she didn't have enough..."

I remained silent.

"I'm going to tell Aunt Elena and Uncle Fabio," he continued, "and then I'm going to phone Cartagena."

I shrugged my shoulders.

He was annoyed by my attitude. "What are our aunt and uncle going to say?"

"Go on, go tell them. Hurry up and explain to them how different we are, and how ashamed you are to be my brother."

"Listen, things can't go on like this. Since you are incapable of telling the truth, I have to do it."

"Of course, the hero."

My aunt was very upset. My uncle said it didn't matter, things like this happened. My mother cried a lot, according to Homero, and asked him to put me on the phone, but I refused. My mother decided that I had to leave for Cartagena. Uncle Fabio promised her that he would buy me a plane ticket.

I had three days left in Bogota.

That night I heard Homero get up and open the window. It seemed to be a clear night. He stood there, looking at the stars for a long while. He closed the window and went back to bed. Later I heard him sobbing.

Two days later I had recuperated and got up. My cousin Ester was waiting for me at the bottom of the stairs with a smile of great triumph. How I would have liked to rip her shirt and bite those tits of hers. Bite them until she cried from pain, until she asked me for forgiveness, until she told me to do whatever I wanted with her. How I would have liked to. But no. I would never dare. That night I would go to the bathroom to masturbate while thinking of all the things that I would like to do to my cousin Ester.

After breakfast I went out for a walk. I headed toward Caracas Avenue and then northward. Without realizing when or how, I found myself in El Chico. El Polo Club was on the other side of the freeway. What a contrast! If the distributing house had not been a failure we would have moved to El Chico, and then.... If the petrochemical plant had not.., we would live in Bocagrande, my father would not have died, I would study nuclear physics in the United States, I would feel love, hate, all sorts of emotion...I would be happy.

Cartagena. The Bay of Cartagena. The Caribbean Sea. My father and I on a motorboat ride to Bocachica. Blue water, blue sky. Beaches, palm trees, light, warmth, life.

I remembered bitterly that we again lived in Cartagena, in the house that my grandfather had bought in Bocagrande. But it was different now. My father would not be waiting for me at the airport.

The Bogota sky started turning gray.

When I was still a boarder at El Calasanz, I had a foreboding that my life was going to fall apart. That was when I learned that my father had sold our new house in Santa Ana. The new house in which we had not yet lived.

It took me an additional hour to get to Santa Ana. I found the house in the middle of willows, pines, and eucalyptus. The neighborhood resembled a forest, or a park at the very least.

I stopped in front of the house. It was one of those designs that Le Courbusier had made common in the northern part of Bogota: modern, sleek, comfortable. It was large, but no more than a home should be. A very well-kept garden graced the space between the trees and the house itself. A little girl was playing with a ball in front of the garage. I felt that someone was observing me. I continued watching the girl with the ball. A few minutes later a maid came out, picked the girl up and carried her into the house. Before closing the door the maid looked at me apprehensively. She thought that I was a burglar. Or who knows what.

The wind picked up the dry leaves and turned them over everywhere. The clouds were painted black.

I began the long walk back.

I had recounted to myself the events of the last four years. I already knew how things had happened. But I still did not know why. But what kind of answer did I want?

What did I mean by "why"? Did I want to know the reason? Or was it, rather, the famous question about the meaning of life? In this case, of my life.

I heard a clap of thunder. And then another.

The reason for my existence. The meaning of my life. But I did not believe in an order that justified everything, in which everything had an assigned place, a meaning. The idea of an infinite design for the benefit of human beings was not.... There were no "reasons." There were no "meanings of life." And if there were none, why should I ask which was mine? I could not find the answer, the great answer, because the question made no sense!

The wind became furious. The leaves began to skitter along the street.

But was that really my question? I only wanted to know why I was dead inside. I only wanted to understand, understand, in order to change, in order to feel again...

The following day I would leave for Cartagena. Cartagena. The fortified walls. The bay. A motorboat in the bay. And my father and I in it. "The career that you want...abroad." The blue sea. Blue. The following day I would leave for Cartagena. I would get off the plane. I would feel the heat's embrace. I would look at the people gathered there. I would look at them as if searching for someone. But my father would not be there. He would never be there. The Bogota sky thundered with fury. I felt a drop sliding down my cheek.

Was it rain?

Born in Barranquilla, Colombia, Gonzalo Munevar emigrated to the United States in 1965. Following four years of service in the Air Force, he earned a Ph.D. in philosophy of science at the University of California at Berkeley. He has since pursued an academic career that has taken him to universities in Australia, Japan, Scotland, and Spain for purposes of research and teaching, as well as Stanford University, the University of Washington, Evergreen State College, the University of California at Irvine, and Lawrence Technological University in Michigan. He became a U.S. citizen in 1969.

At the age of eighteen he began publishing short stories, poetry, and literary criticism in his native Colombia. He has published over 30 academic papers and given more than 100 professional talks around the world. He is the author of *Radical Knowledge* and *Evolution and the Naked Truth*. He is currently finishing two books in philosophy: *The Dimming of Starlight: The Philosophy of Space Exploration* and *A Theory of Wonder*. He is the editor of *Spanish Studies in the Philosophy of Science, Beyond Reason,* and (with D. Lamb and J. Preston) *The Worst Enemy of Science? The Master of Fate* is his first novel. He is at work on another novel.